FINALLY IN FOCUS

FINALLY IN FOCUS

NAOMI SPRINGTHORP

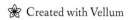 Created with Vellum

Sometimes we all need to stop and let the world around us come into focus.

CHAPTER 1

There's nothing like the warmth of sunshine on my face as I leave work on Friday afternoon. Finally, free for my weekend and away from the boring stuffed shirts I work with. I'm light on my feet as I twirl my way across the parking lot to my car. I turn the radio up for the drive home and relax, happily singing at the top of my lungs and trying to settle into my weekend. I get home to find Mark sitting on the stairs to my place and the wind suddenly disappears from my sails.

Shouldn't I be happy he's at my apartment waiting for me? I'm guessing my wish he would forget about me and not be here when I get home isn't the norm for people who have been dating exclusively for years. His presence doesn't put a smile on my face or kick-start my heart. I simply wonder why he's here. He's always at my place on Friday after work and Saturday after his poker game. He texts me a few times during the week, but Sundays are reserved for his precious golf game, and Monday through Thursday are dedicated to watching sports, sleep, the bar with the guys—everything except me. Yet, I know he's going to be groping me as soon as I'm within his reach.

I don't consider Mark my boyfriend, he's comfortable and kind of dependable. He started asking me out in college and he was nice to look at. It made sense to give him a shot after I had settled into my job. Logically, the next step would be to find a man, and at some point get married. It's what's expected.

He follows me up the stairs to my apartment above my parent's garage and holds himself to my back while I unlock the door, pressing his cock to my ass. "Wanna have some fun, baby?"

I release an exasperated sigh in response and step into my apartment. He has his shirt off before he can walk across my living room. His shoes and socks create a path to my bedroom, and I pick up his mess on my way to change out of my work clothes. I grab clean clothes and lock myself in my bathroom. I'm tired of this shit and I need some alone time. Maybe it would be different if Mark were like this everyday, giving me attention and wanting to spend time with me. Instead, he comes to me for sex, and only on the weekends. I don't know if he's been conditioned somehow by something in his life or what. Honestly, I'm not interested anymore. I spend as long as possible in the shower, taking the time to use my special conditioner, apply my facial mask, and listen to the whole playlist I have programmed on my phone.

I find Mark sitting on my couch in his boxers with a game on the TV. "You get all cleaned up for me, baby?"

I ignore him and peruse my kitchen in search of dinner.

"Olivia?"

"Will you give me a break? I just got home from work and I need to unwind." The words come out bitchier than I had intended. I was ready for the weekend until I found him waiting for me. I don't have anything planned, but I was looking forward to time away from the office and sleeping in.

"I know how to help you with that, but you need to take those clothes off and come sit on my lap."

It's the same every Friday. He always expects to get whatever he wants and acts like I should be wandering about naked, bringing him beer or whatever delight he desires. He doesn't greet me with a kiss, he greets me with his dick. I focus on him sitting in my living room and all I can see is a selfish jerk who probably jacked off while I was in the shower. He'd love it if I'd give him a lap dance. That'll never happen.

We usually end up ordering delivery or I have to cook on Friday night. I brown bag my lunch, but Friday is the exception to the rule and I go out to lunch. It's my splurge. It gets me through the end of the week without killing anybody. I have leftovers from my favorite Mexican food place and they're calling my name. I plop down on my couch with my reheated leftovers in hand and snatch the remote, surfing the channels until I find something I want to watch. I start with game shows while I consider what I want to binge watch.

"I was watching the game," he objects loudly to my choice with his mad man voice, but it doesn't faze me. I don't give two shits about it.

"I told you I need to unwind and you know I don't watch sports." I glare at him and roll my eyes, silently adding *you idiot* to my comment.

He groans under his breath and continues, "Where's my plate?"

"I only have enough leftovers for me. I figured you ate already since you didn't bring food or offer to take me out or anything."

I watched him while he ordered a pizza for delivery. More specifically, a pizza with the toppings I won't eat. The extremely minimal chance of him getting laid tonight dropped to zero with him eating anchovies.

———

Saturday morning is beautiful when I wake up alone. Apparently, Mark got a clue and went home when I went to bed last night.

I've been living in the apartment above my parent's garage rent-free since I turned 20. I'm more a caretaker than anything else. I make sure the yard is kept and it looks like someone is home while they travel for work and go on vacations. Technically, my rent is the $100 I pay the yard guy each month, watering plants, feeding fish, bringing in mail and maintaining their finances—yes, I'm in charge of their bills and I give my parents each an allowance. I've always been better with money and they get everything they want this way without stress. Of course, paying their bills is also keeping my water on. I volunteered for the task after my water had been shut off, then my wifi, and then the electricity. Every month I was going days without a warm shower or some other creature comfort. I might as well have been camping inside my apartment. It's much better this way. I'm the responsible adult.

It all makes perfect sense. Completely logical, well-balanced adult life.

I hate it.

I don't know if it's Mark or my job. I know it's not my apartment because my parents are never home anyway. I need a change and it's going to take more than a haircut to satisfy me. I'm in a rut and I need something different. I don't know what I want.

Okay, I could be lying. Kade Bloch. I want Kade. I've wanted him since high school, but it made no sense to be interested in a guy who never went to class and always had extra cash. What teenager ever had extra cash? It had to be bad news or illegal. His overgrown light brown hair hanging down into his eyes. His T-shirts were worn, old, and faded, sometimes not long enough to meet the jeans at his waist, and always stretched perfectly across his shoulders. He wore old school button-fly jeans, none of those relaxed fit or skinny jeans or anything stylish, and in fact he still wears those, but now it's usually topped with a black polo shirt (varying degrees of black, since it appears he doesn't care if they fade). Yes, I saw him recently. Shit. I see him all the time. Fine. I know where to find him when I want a glimpse. He's predictable and I'm good with patterns. I haven't spoke to him since senior ditch day, which was the longest conversation I've ever had with him. He had surprised me with his passion and intelligence. He hated school and the drama of everything it encompassed. He was on the home study program, but spent most of his time in the photography lab on campus. I remember learning about his schedule and being hit with my misconception, he wasn't ditching at all. I admired his mouth when he talked to me, and his hands as he used them to describe his words. He had passion in his hands when he held his camera and creativity shining in his hazel eyes. Yeah, I've dreamt about Kade since ditch day. What would it feel like for those hands to touch me? Would his mouth kiss with the same passion?

I need a distraction, maybe a reality check. I can't get Kade out of my head and I know Mark will be by after his Saturday night poker game. It'll be the same as every other Saturday night. He'll bring us an unhealthy and deliciously tasty midnight snack, possibly a six pack of something fruity and alcoholic, and want to get laid. Yep, the rut—would we be sharing the steak sandwich dinner from the burger place? Or would it be ice cream with French fries tonight? For some reason that I've never been able to determine (other than he's stereotyping me a typical girl), Mark thinks I only drink sparkling alcoholic beverages, and what he brings over will tell me how much he wants to get laid, or maybe more accurately, how much he wants me.

It's a warm summer evening and I go for a walk through the neighborhood, admiring the leaves on the trees hanging like a canopy over the street I grew up on. The streetlights are glowing intermittently between them and buzzing as they each come on for the night. The breeze blowing through to play with the leaves, refreshes me and hopefully is getting my head in the right place.

I keep walking until I get to the old downtown area. I haven't been here on a weekend evening in years. I take a personal tour noticing refurbishments the town has made to honor its history and be energy efficient, while maintaining its unique charm and personality. The main drag with a park-like walkway down the middle of the street is lit with pot lights planted in the ground and white LEDs in the trees. The sidewalks are lined with signs from businesses on both sides of the street. I'd never noticed how many neon signs there were. Everything from "open," "free delivery" and "we never close" to custom signs like "Tony's Pizza," and "Bloch Photography" hanging in an upstairs window with the lights on. I admit I'm tempted to investigate. I gaze at the window. Does Kade have a gallery up there? A Studio? Both? I didn't know he had a business, let alone that he's still into photography. I maintain my curiosity with plans to research Bloch Photography online. I do an about face and walk back toward my neighborhood using the walkway in the center of the street.

The lights make me happy, almost joyous like a child at an amusement park and add a bounce to my step. I get about halfway down the walk and it's blocked by a man lying on the ground. He's facing away from me on his belly with his feet bottoms-up and pointed straight at me. He's wearing a faded black baseball cap backwards. His elbows are pointed out from his sides, like wings at his large muscled shoulders. He doesn't appear to be homeless, hurt, or in danger. I don't have a clue why anyone would choose to lie on the sidewalk. Face up maybe to admire the lights, maybe pretend you're in a fantasy world, but not face down. I hesitate and consider moving to the side of the road to avoid the crazy person lying in my path, but this time my curiosity wins.

I walk up behind him. "Hey, you okay? Did you drop something small?" My voice is tentative and the rapid beat of my heart makes me question who's making decisions for me today.

There's an audible irritated, caveman-like grunt, then quietly, "Just stay where you are, be quiet, and don't move for a couple minutes."

I do as he asks. I stand there, picturing a scene from a horror flick where the serial killer in a clown mask chases the woman through the center of town with a machete. I should turn around and run, but there's something familiar about his voice.

A few minutes pass, "Sorry about that, just give me a second to set this up on time-lapse." He stands up, pulling his tall frame up off the ground and turns to face me.

Kade is standing in front of me, all sexy man. This is the last thing I need. Not a distraction. Absolute opposite of a distraction. Suddenly I'm in high school again and it's senior ditch day. I can't help but appreciate his hands and his mouth, wanting to experience them both personally. Is he the same as he was then? He's more rugged and moves with comfort in his own skin, confident and sexy. His eyes are clear and sparkling with gold flecks as he takes me in from head to toe.

"Olivia? I thought I saw you the other day near the coffee shop." He reaches out to me, pulling me in for a quick and friendly hug.

I smile at him in agreement, afraid of what words will come out of my mouth to no doubt fail me at this moment. The smell of him and the heat of his body surround me, bombarding my senses. "Kade? Wow! I didn't recognize you." Dumb. Dumb. Dumb. Because you would recognize the bottoms of his soled shoes? Maybe his head with a cap on it? I guess I'd be a stalker if I recognized his ass from the rear view. Hurray! I'm not a stalker. "Why were you lying on the ground?"

"What are you doing here by yourself?"

"I'm walking back home. Not too concerned, we basically live in Mayberry." Though I did narrowly escape an incident involving a clown and a machete. Close one. Sarcasm took over my brain, but I managed to keep my mouth shut and not make a fool of myself in front of Kade.

"Let me get this set-up secured and I'll walk with you."

Who am I to argue? I watch as he skillfully secures a couple small cameras in different places on either side of the walkway, one on the ground and another in a tree. He turns to me and smiles, like what he's doing is completely normal.

I wait curiously, unable to take my eyes off him. "So, why were you lying on the ground?"

"Oh, yeah, a few different things. I volunteered to solve the problem the city is having with the lighting on the walkway. It's squirrels. I need to figure out where they're accessing the wires or where they've decided the best place is to snack on wires. Most of the wiring already has protective covering. I'm taking advantage of the project to work on my time-lapse photography skills, and I'm attracted to the view of the lighting from the different angles. It gives me an abstract sense of being in a fantasy. Anyway, it's an interesting subject matter, I'm trying to combine it with the movement of the headlights driving by and the neon signs."

"That's only two, not a few." Why did I say that? Can't I be nice and not critical for five measly minutes?

He chuckles, "Squirrels are cute and furry. Squirrel photos remind me of camping with my family when I was younger. My aunt always had pictures to show from trips and nobody could see what the subject was. It was a squirrel. The original Where's Waldo pictures." He smiles bright at his memory.

"Squirrels are fun." I try not to talk more than necessary and it's easy because all I can do is imagine him holding me close while he presses his lips to mine. I'm hot all over and my blood is racing. I've never experienced this level of need and desire, not even during sex. Mark gets the job done, sometimes, but he doesn't have a passionate bone in his body. Kade is sex on a stick and if he has half the passion for me as he has for his photography, I may never leave the house again.

Our eyes meet and fire burns through me. He touches my cheek, his hand gentle and strong. "You look flushed. Are you feeling okay?"

"I'm fine. Probably just the warm weather." Or you, Mr. Sexy Photographer. Suddenly I find myself imagining him with his camera focused on me. "You must be taking photos of something else besides squirrels. I saw Bloch Photography on the second floor above the diner."

This embarrassed almost bashful expression crosses his face, "I photograph anything and everything. Portraits, headshots, commissioned projects, and I do some photojournalism. I prefer my own projects, but I have found other things trigger personal projects and research for me."

Without thinking, "Do you shoot nudes? I mean, models?"

He laughs, "I have. I get calls for photo shoots and sometimes they're nudes. Nudes aren't always what you assume. Usually what people consider artistic, not hot and sexy." His tone tells me he's seen things he wishes he could forget. He flits his eyes around exploring my face and features. "I'd like to get you in front of my camera. Not nude, not that you would be bad nude. I mean, I'm sure you'd be hot and sexy. I'm going to shut up now."

His tongue is as bad as mine. I giggle at him and wish I had the nerve to touch his cheek, but I don't. I manage a smile and turn to walk up to my apartment.

He grabs my hand sending tingles up my arm. "Hey, have a good night."

"You too."

He releases my hand and turns away as he scrubs his hand through his hair. I go upstairs quickly to keep myself from doing something stupid and watch him from my window with my teenage girl eyes as he walks down the street. It's a great view, and I see him turn around to look back.

CHAPTER 2

I sit down at my computer and search Kade Bloch. I can't
believe I've never searched him before. It's confirmed: I'm not
a stalker. I find photos of him with a camera in his hand, his business profile, a webpage for his business, show announcements,
social media with his name all over it and photos. Photos of everything from everywhere—Protests, cars, newspaper articles, magazine spreads, weddings, war, landscapes, portraits, models, our
town, and, of course, squirrels.

Forget not being a stalker. I'm a complete fail! How have I
crushed on a guy for so many years and not known what he was
doing when he was so prevalent and available to be searched? All
I did was type in his name and hit enter!

I'm startled by a noise outside. There's someone walking up
my stairs. I've been sitting here googling Kade for hours and now
Mark is here. Not Mark. Not Mark. Not Mark! I can't deal with
him right now. All I can do is envision how I'd like to *Google*
Kade and wish for nude shots of him, about the only thing I
didn't find. I can't have Mark here right now. It's not going to
happen. It can't happen. Get it together quick, Olivia. The door

is locked, the lights are off and he can't see me sitting at my computer in my bedroom. He'll want to know where I am if I don't answer and probably call me. I'm not a liar.

There's knocking at my door. "Hey baby, it's me." Yep, Mark.

Slowly I move toward the door, hoping he might leave before I get there. "I'm not feeling well. Probably not a good time."

"I should come in and make sure you're okay."

"I'm fine, it's just..." think quick, think quick and make it good, "...girlie issues."

"Oh, you need anything?"

"No, I have everything I need."

"Feel better, baby." His footsteps clomp back down the stairs. Technically, I didn't lie—I'm definitely having some type of girlie issue, the Kade Bloch type.

I was with Kade all weekend—Mentally, not physically. He had no idea. I had dreams about him and the dreams were better than real life with Mark. I woke up hot and sweaty more than once. I was wet all night long and I never believed wet dreams existed. They most certainly do.

Mark left me alone for the rest of the weekend because he assumed my girlie issues would make me unavailable for sex. I'm not complaining. It was the best weekend I've had in a long time.

———

It's Monday morning. I'm up early, refreshed and ready for work. I'm ready for my special treat coffee. I'm not a whack job, I hate Mondays like everyone else. I stop to get my coffee and run into Kade. Physically, with hot coffee in his hand. "I'm so sorry. Let me help." I pull napkins from the dispenser on the counter and start dabbing at him to dry him off, but all it does is make me wet.

He grins at me, "It's fine. I can go change. Takes more than spilled coffee to ruin my day. It's not like it's, I don't know, spilled milk or anything."

"I'll get you another coffee."

"Don't worry about it. I gotta get up to my office." He takes off quickly.

I order my coffee and get him a replacement. I'd have to take it up to him. I have a few minutes extra, I allow myself extra time in the morning. I get to work almost twenty minutes early every-day, it allows for delays and plenty of time for me to be polite with my co-workers.

I climb the stairs to his office with coffee in hand and knock.

"Come on in."

I walk through the door and I'm surrounded by enlarged prints of his photos, some large enough to fill a whole wall. All of them staggering in tone and color, mostly abstract or macro, not his magazine work. "Wow. I brought you coffee." I call out to get his location.

"Back here in the corner by the window."

I'm walking through a maze of hanging photos, different sizes, different colors, all suspended by thin cables. He'd made his entry his personal gallery and it's beautiful. I finally find the cheese at the end of the maze. Kade is sitting at his computer editing a photo with the sunlight shining in the window behind him. His view and the view of him are both staggering.

"You didn't have to bring me coffee. Thank you."

"I did. I basically made your Monday even better by drenching you in your own coffee."

"This is the best Monday morning I've had in a long time." He held my eyes with his and butterflies fluttered low in my belly.

Keep it together, Olivia, "I don't know how that's possible. I'm off to work, so you don't have to worry about being assaulted with a donut or anything."

"Donuts sound good."

"What kind do you like? The kind with a hole in the middle or the long ones?" Why did it sound so dirty in my head?

"I like glazed ones with a hole in the middle." He says it with a straight face, so I know he doesn't mean it the way I hear it. I need to have a conversation with my wet and wishful hole to help it understand.

"I'll remember for future reference. Have a better day."

"Not possible, there's no way it gets better than this." I start to walk away with visions in my head of ways it could get better and he calls after me. "Olivia?"

"Yeah?"

"I'm going out on site to do a shoot tomorrow, gorgeous location. Are you interested in going with me?"

"Sure." I call back over my shoulder and get out before I do anything else stupid, since it appears I will be calling in sick tomorrow.

———

I daydream about Kade all day. Did he invite me to his shoot like a date or because he needs help? I hope he's not getting back at me for spilling coffee on him, and taking me someplace horrid which requires hiking in the hot summer sun or possibly has creepy insects. I have no idea where this stupid girl in me is coming from. But, I'm anxious for time with Kade. I manage to get my work done, so I can call in sick tomorrow without being missed too much. Unfortunately, karma is a bitch and I'm pulled over at the side of the road puking my guts out before I can get home from work.

Karma in my head, "Planning on calling in sick, huh? I can help you with that. <Poof> Now, you're sick."

Damn it.

I pull over three times on my way home and I get home almost two hours later than usual. Miserable and challenged by the simple task of climbing up my stairs, I get myself settled and call in sick. I find the number to Bloch Photography and call, mad at the world for taking my day with Kade away from me.

"Bloch Photography." It's him, and I didn't expect him to answer at this time of night.

"Hi, this is Olivia."

"Hi," he sounds happy to hear from me. "I didn't think I'd talk to you until tomorrow."

"About that, I'm sick. I can't make it."

"I understand. I'll reschedule the shoot when you are better. What's wrong?"

"I don't know. I puked up stuff I don't remember eating." Feeling sorry for myself and wanting to take the words back, so I could talk to him about something more attractive than vomit. "You don't need to reschedule for me."

"Yes, I do. The location won't be gorgeous without you."

"When did you become a sweet talker?"

"I'm not. I'm a photographer and I know real beauty when I see it."

I giggle at the compliment and I shouldn't have. My stomach rumbles back at me, "I need to go to bed."

"Do you need anything? I'm happy to bring you ginger ale, crackers, drugs, whatever you want."

"No, I don't want to get you sick. Thank you." I also don't want you to see me like this because I'm pretty sure I look like crap.

"Would you mind if I call to check on you later?"

"That might be nice." I can't help the smile spreading across my face and taking over my cheeks. The sound of happiness in my voice traveling to his ears.

"Yeah? If you're feeling better, maybe we can talk for a while. Call if you need anything."

"Thanks. Bye." I hang up, holding my phone to my heart and close my eyes.

I wake up about 3am to text messages.

Mom - It's after 10pm and I haven't heard from you today. Please check in.

Kade - Hope you're feeling better. I didn't want to call and wake you up. Call me when you wake up.

Mark - It's after midnight and your Mom is trying to find you. Call her or something so she will leave me alone.

Mark - It's 2am, where are you?

To Mom - Sorry, sick and fell asleep. I'll be okay.

To Mark - I'm sick. Why are you up at 2am?

Mom - I'm sorry. Do you want me to come home and take care of you?

To Mom - I'll be fine. You don't need to.

Mark - ...

Mark - Sleeping now.

Mark - Horny, how about you?

Asshole.

To Mark - I told you I'm sick

Mark - That was Friday

To Mark - Puking today

Mom - If you're sure. Call if you want me to come home. Love you

To Kade - I just woke up. Are you awake?

CHAPTER 3

My phone rang instantly, "Hello?"

"Hi, how are you feeling?" Kade's voice is kind and caring.

"I don't know. I'm awake, so I'm not dead and that's good."

He chuckles, "I can't argue with that."

"Why are you still up?"

"My plans for tomorrow got canceled, so I decided to work late. I'm going through photos to update my portfolio and doing some editing."

"Sorry your plans got canceled."

"It's okay. I was hoping to get this woman I'm interested in to do a photo shoot for me. I always see people more clearly through the lens of my camera. It's almost automatic, I match people with locations. It's something about the colors and the elements."

"What about me?" I question, not sure if I should be mad or hurt.

"What do you mean?"

"You were taking me with you to help take photos of the woman you're interested in?"

"You're her, Olivia." His voice is warm, soft and something else I can't decipher.

"Oh," his words zing through me.

"Are you taken?"

I can't lie to Kade and I don't want to tell him the truth. "I've been dating a guy for a while, but he's not my boyfriend."

"Does he give you what you need?"

"No."

"Why are you still dating him?"

"I don't know. I avoid him sometimes."

"Do you feel special when he touches you?"

"No."

"When he kisses you, does it make you want more?"

"Not unless I've been drinking."

His voice low and rough, "Does he take care of you the way you deserve to be taken care of when he loves you?"

"He doesn't love me. I'm not sure what I deserve."

"Olivia, is it only him or is there somebody else?"

"There might be somebody else who makes me desire more, makes me want things when he simply walks with me, talks with me. I'm not sure yet."

"Olivia, you should never settle. If there's not passion, if he doesn't physically need to be with you and touch you, don't waste your time. I've seen things in my travels and you should never waste time with the wrong person or anyone who doesn't really care for you."

I remind myself about how Mark only shows up on the weekends and when he wants sex. How I've allowed our dating to morph into this fuck buddy on the weekend relationship. I'm done. "You're right. It's been over, I need to end it and haven't done it."

"What about the other guy?"

"It's nothing yet. I want his hands on me and I want to taste his mouth on mine. I've dreamt about it and I need it." I've lost my mind. Should I blame the time of day or my illness for my free words?

"Tell me about him."

"He's an artist and full of passion. Passion I'm missing in my life. His strong, gentle hands treat everything like a piece of art."

"Maybe you're like a valuable piece of art to him and he doesn't treat everything or anyone else like you. Maybe it's how he feels about you."

"I doubt it. I don't have his passion. He's merely an acquaintance. The sensation when his hand brushes against mine is unlike any other I've experienced, but everything else has only been dreams—real to me, and not to him."

"You need the right man to bring out your passion. When he touches your hand, do you feel it like an electrical current through your body? Does it make you want his touch?"

"Yes."

"And, when he kisses you?"

"He's only kissed me in my dreams and when he does, I have to have him completely."

"Do you dream about..."

"He holds me close and kisses me tenderly as he takes me. He's in complete control and sends me out of this world. When he holds my naked body tightly against him, he's going to take me harder and I can't wait. He handles me perfectly. The pleasure shines in his eyes and his entire body hums at our connection. I'm his and would do anything for him. Everything is him." My eyes are closed and I surprise myself talking through my dream with such desire in my voice. "I'm sorry, I'm falling asleep."

His voice low, "You need to get back to sleep. Has anyone in your life been like your dream?"

"Nobody."

"Any possibility I could be?"

"Kade, I shouldn't say this, but you're the one in the dream."

"Yeah? Maybe someday you'll allow me to show you my passion for something besides my photography?"

"I hope you want to someday."

"Olivia, know I want you. Get rid of that guy who doesn't deserve you and let me show you what it's like to live."

I giggle.

"Now I'm going to think you're dreaming of me and I want to dream of you."

"I will be dreaming of you." The smile on my face projected in my voice.

"Goodnight, Olivia," His tone soft and sexy.

I wish I could watch and participate in his dreams.

"Goodnight." I hang up and fall back asleep already in dreamland.

My dreams are vivid, clearer than ever before. His words full of desire at my ear and his arms around me, holding me against him. His want and need for me rolling off him in waves. My heartbeat in my ears drowning out everything else. I want him badly and his passion is overwhelming. How can he hold me so dearly, loving me, caressing me, taking care of me and somehow manage to overflow my emotions with even more love when he takes me deep and hard? I'm crying out his name in need and I've never cried out to anyone. His mouth on mine muffling my cries and claiming me as his own, conveying how he won't be sharing me with anyone. His full soft lips pressing against mine repeatedly and his tongue dancing with mine like a couple that was born to tango together. The passion between us building and our heat an inferno, we explode together and our world is on fire, flames combusting and exploding at every turn. His arms around me keep me safe and protected as we recover together and he whispers sweet nothings passionately in my ear. His words are hot and loving, lustful and needy. His words are an echo of my own as they pound through my heart and I want more.

I wake up Tuesday in the middle of the afternoon. My stomach isn't rolling and my head is no longer ready to spin off. I'm struck with the memory of my dreams. I want his warm breath at my ear with his sweet words, whispering to me the way he did in my dreams. It's crazy and no more than a dream, not at all how things are in real life. Guys aren't like that. They don't connect like that, they're all about wanting to get their rocks off. If I go strictly by Mark, I'd say they're selfish bastards and only get chicks off because they want to fuck them again. Yeah, my dreams are completely fabricated from the female psyche and there's no way any man is like that. Don't get wrapped up in your imagination and the traits you have put on your crush, Olivia. He's still a man. He will hit it and quit it. He has girls everywhere. He probably has a girlfriend or maybe he's married, though I didn't find anything like that on my Google quest. He's nothing but a sweet talker. He's nice to look at, but he will break you. It's true, Kade can break me and I should stay away. The fact he's probably not as passionate and sexually adept as I dream he is drives me to want to find out. If he isn't what I've imagined, he'll be easy to forget.

I check my phone and a text pops through.

Kade - How are you feeling? Are you awake yet?

To Kade - Just woke up. Better I think, but not great.

Kade - :)

Kade - Sorry about our conversation last night. I shouldn't have gone there. No excuses.

To Kade - I had the best dream last night

Kade - Stop, Olivia. Why are you bringing it back up?

To Kade - I liked it. Did you dream about me?

Kade - You need your rest

He's gone. Just like that? I don't get it.

A few minutes later my phone rings, "Hello?"

"There's a delivery at your door. I promise it's not me. I left you a care package."

"Okay." I'm aware of everyone who climbs my stairs. What kind of ninja is he to get up my stairs without me catching him?

"Will you go out with me Friday night?"

Mark always shows up on Friday after work, but it doesn't matter because I won't be here. "Sounds great. I hope I'm up to it by then."

"Good. I'll let you go and you can get your package."

"Okay. Thank you."

"See you Friday." He hangs up.

I slowly get out of bed and go through my first thing in the morning routine. I open my door to find a bag from the diner and a bouquet of Stargazer Lilies. I smile at the flowers and as I turn to go back inside, I catch a glimpse of Kade standing on the curb. I wave and he waves back before he walks off toward his office. The flowers have a card...

Olivia,

I hope you said yes. These are a clue about what we will be doing Friday night. Feel better soon.

Kade

I open the bag from the diner to find a bottle of 7Up, a bag of assorted donut holes and a to-go container filled with toast. White toast, wheat toast, and English muffins.

I call him, "Bloch Photography."

"Thank you. The care package is perfect." I laugh and continue, "I prefer bars to holes."

"Olivia, you make me..." Kade's voice changes, lower and thicker, "I could only focus on the holes."

"Oh," Fuck me. Donuts will never be the same. I couldn't help myself, "I like the ones with nuts, too." It's true, not just innuendo.

"Liv," oh my god that sounds sexy from his lips, "I just want to hold your hand and hang out."

I giggle and fantasize about how I will respond to him in person. My dreams are so real. I want, no, I need his lips pressed to mine and the heat of his body near me. Will he be like in my dreams or is it all a figment of my imagination?

"I like that happy sound. It reminds me of a picture I found last night. I'll send it to you when I get to my office."

"Did you take the long walk back?" I laugh and completely forget I'm sick.

"No," he hesitates, "I stopped to sit on the curb because I turned around and started walking back to you."

"You shouldn't do that. You don't want to get sick. I'm a mess."

"I'm aware. I'm staying away and talking to you instead. You were flushed when I saw you Friday, but glowing on Monday."

I want to tell him it was all him, but I don't. He's so easy to say anything to. I don't have a need to hide anything from him, I want him to know everything.

"Go eat, so you get better. I'll text you the picture."

"Okay, bye." I hang up, but all I really want to do is talk to Kade. Fine, that's a lie. All I really want to do is have him naked in my bed with his mouth all over me. Something must be wrong with me. Oh right, I'm sick.

I gnaw on my toast slowly and sip 7Up with a straw straight from the bottle. I call to check in with my mom.

"Hello?"

"Hey, Mom. I'm feeling a little better. I'm calling since I'm finally awake."

"Good. I'm happy to hear it, Livi. A sick day or two isn't always a bad thing. How is everything going?"

Sometimes I forget my mom is an excellent listener and knows I'm not a kid. "What do you think about Mark?"

"What are you getting at?"

"Do you think I can do better?"

"You're my daughter and you deserve the best. If you're questioning it, move on."

"Thanks, Mom."

"Is there somebody else?"

"I'm not sure yet, maybe. He's taking me on a date Friday night."

"I'm always here if you want to talk. Call in sick for tomorrow. Relax and make sure you're better, okay?"

"I've got weeks of sick time, I will call in for tomorrow right now. Talk soon. Thanks."

To Mark - I'm feeling a bit better today, not that you asked.

I'm in a bitchy mood, I'm going with it and blaming it on being sick.

I wait for him to respond to my text, but he doesn't.

To Mark - We need to talk.

Mark - Why are you texting me during your work day? You never do that.

To Mark - I'm at home sick, jackass.

Mark - What's up?

To Mark - This isn't a text conversation

Mark - Are you knocked up?

Mark - It's not mine. I always use a condom.

Talk about confirmation on my decision. What if I was pregnant? He'd deny it even though he's the only man I've been with.

To Mark - No. Good to know how you would handle that.

To Mark - I guess it would be Immaculate Conception and not a faulty rubber then since you're the only guy I've been with.

Mark - You know that's not what I meant

Do I? No, I really don't.

To Mark - We need to talk.

Mark - Okay. I'll be there early on Friday and we can talk.

To Mark - We need to talk today. Now would be best.

My phone starts ringing and the caller ID tells me it's Mark. "Hi, so why wait until Friday when you could call me so quickly?"

"The guys are waiting on me. What's up?" he sounds irritated and rushed.

"Can you come by for a few minutes, so we can talk?"

"You horny, baby? I can be there in a jiffy."

"No, not so much."

"Well, I'm kinda busy this week, so it can wait until Friday or we can talk on the phone."

Busy unless he gets laid. Sounds about right. "Okay, it's not going to work out. It's all me. It would be best if we go our separate ways and move on with our lives."

"Wait, what?"

"You don't want to spend time with me unless you're getting laid. Honestly, I don't want to spend time with you. We should be done."

"Are you breaking up with me?" Sounding bewildered.

"We broke up a long time ago. We're a scheduled hook-up now."

"What about me? What about us?" Suddenly he's paying attention.

"We both know all you want is sex. I'm sure you can find someone else to ply with alcohol that will give it up."

"You're breaking up with me. I can't believe it. I'm the best thing that ever happened to you. You should think carefully before you break up with me."

"Can you break up with a fuck buddy?"

"It's not like that and you know you want me. You love what I do to you."

"No, I don't and it's all pretty one-sided if you ask me. I can't remember the last time I got mine."

"Did you get another promotion? Now I'm not good enough for you?"

"At least you got one part of that right... and I didn't get another promotion."

"Frigid bitch. Fuck you."

I hang up on him. That should do it. I don't think I've been this free and happy in years.

CHAPTER 4

A photo from Kade pops through and it takes me back to ditch day. Nobody has ever shared this photo with me before and it makes me happy all over. It's Kade and I leaning against a tree together on senior ditch day. Memories of the day are vivid. I can almost smell the scent of his shampoo, light and fresh. Our legs were stretched out, my foot leaned over to his leg and we were sitting close, hip-to-hip. I don't remember his arm being around me, but it was draped across my shoulders. Maybe we were posing for the photo. He had his camera in his other hand, taking a photo of us together at the same time. The expressions on our faces tell the story, we were comfortable yet unsure sitting there together. There should be thought bubbles above our heads filled with our hormone driven teenage ideas.

Kade: This chick is cool. I wonder if she likes me. I really want to kiss her. I should ask her out. Man, I want to pull her closer to me.

Me: I didn't know he's smart. Kinda makes me want him. He's hot. I wish he would kiss me.

To Kade - I love the photo. I've never seen it before. Where's the photo you were taking?
Kade - It's been photoshopped. I don't have the original anymore.
To Kade - You don't want me to see it?
Kade - It was a long time ago
To Kade - Just send it to me

What did he do? Put a beard on me? Give me a mohawk? X out my eyes? The photo popped through and I...

To Kade - Did you photoshop it?

There's no answer. He's probably talking to a client. It doesn't matter, it might as well be rhetorical. The photo is black and white, the edges have been softened and the tree has been photoshopped with K+O in the middle of a heart carved above our heads. He's proud to have his arm around me and I'm focused on him like he's the only one who matters. How did I miss this then? Have we been crushing on each other this whole time?

To Kade - We never talked about you. Do you have a girl?

A few minutes later...

Kade - I photoshopped it back then, before I learned to keep the original of everything.

To Kade - It's perfect.

Kade - :)

Kade - <3

Kade - The only girl is you

To Kade - The only guy is you

My phone rings instantly, "Hello?"

"Hi, what happened to the guy?"

"I told him I don't want to date him anymore."

"I'm sorry."

"Don't be. I deserve better. Besides, I need a change."

"What do you mean?"

"You'll think I'm crazy."

"Try me."

"I don't like my life. I've always done everything I should do and everything expected of me." I remember how I picked my major logically, thinking about the future and making sure I wouldn't be touching any bedpans or cleaning up any puke or acting as some creep's bitch. "I graduated at the top of my class. I've been methodical, logical, and responsible, always making the safe life choices. I have my MBA, I work for one of the largest companies in the country, I get top notch benefits, I'm paid a decent wage, I have almost no debt, I have a sweet deal for my apartment—always completely logical, sound choices—and I need a change. No clue what, but getting rid of the guy I was dating is definitely a step in the right direction."

"Are you sure you want a man?"

"I only want a man if he's the right one and he wants me, too. I don't need one."

"You've never taken any risks. What do you want to do?"

"I don't know. I've never considered what I want beyond being safe. I've always gone with what's expected of me."

"You're making everyone else happy. What makes you happy?"

I can't say you without being a stupid girl. "I like talking to you."

"I like talking to you, too, but that's not the point. Remember when we were in high school, what did you do for fun in your free time? For instance, I enjoy photography."

"I read a lot and I liked to write in my journal."

"What did you write in your journal?"

"Sometimes it was more like my diary and other times I would write poetry, or make lists of places I wanted to go, or write about why I liked something, or write short stories. It was all very private and I never shared any of it."

"I bet you haven't done any of that since you started college. I remember you liked going out to the park to hang out, the biggest kid on the swings with the wind blowing through your long golden blonde hair and you were in heaven when you were flying on the swings. I remember you sitting on top of the monkey bars reading a book quietly and content to be left alone. You almost always had a book in your pocket. Maybe it's the adulting phenomenon, we forget how to have fun and what it's like to be a kid."

He's right. The long forgotten memory of the wind rushing past me as I swing hard and high, gives me a sense of freedom. Filled with the bold, free spirit of the swings, "I want to kiss you."

"What?" He's surprised at my words.

"In my dream... I believe your kiss will give me the same adrenaline rush as the swings, but better."

"Liv, we shouldn't rush this. I don't want to push you."

"I'm doing the pushing. It's not what I'd planned or hoped for. It's what I want. It's not that we need to move fast, it's that I need to feel our connection. Not dirty, the spark. I want to experience the spark, confirm it's real and waiting for us. I want the passion of my future, I want to know what's waiting for me. Passion like I've never imagined." What the hell has gotten into me?

"Slow down and enjoy the process, you only get to live through it once. I want to kiss you and hold you and so much more. I need to take it slow, I can't dive into the deep end head first. You never know how long it will last and every moment needs to be cherished."

"Who was she?"

He chuckles under his breath, "I had hired her to be my tour guide around Europe. It was my first trip over and I was mostly exploring for myself. There was an immediate mutual attraction when we met and I didn't take any time to learn about who she was or consider what I was doing. I was a young, dumb guy and let my dick lead. I physically needed her. We spent almost five months together traveling through Europe. I was in love with her and she told me she loved me. I believe she did, I could read it in her eyes and it embraced me when we were together, when we made love. One morning I woke to a note telling me to go home because she was going home. She had been pregnant by me and didn't tell me. It was new, maybe only a month or so and she had lost it. We had lost it. She was going to stay with me, but after losing what had started and finding out her husband was getting out of the military, she went home to be there waiting for him. I had no way of contacting her and she was already gone. She had never told me she was married. In my heart, she was mine and there was nobody else. I'm not making that mistake again. I would've stayed in Europe for her or brought her home with me, whatever she wanted. I would've given her whatever she wanted." He stops, his voice had gotten quieter with every word he said. "My flaw to carry now, I'm guarded and careful even when I want something, someone, desperately."

"I'm sorry."

"Please don't be. It's been years now and you make me want to take chances again." The tone of his voice travels through me and I'm struck with fear. What if my passion isn't enough for him? What if I'm not worth him risking his heart? What if I don't feel the spark? What if we want different things? Interesting, since I don't have a clue what I want. Fine, I want him naked. But, that's not what I meant and you know it. It's expected I get married and have a family. I'm not making choices based on expectations anymore.

"Kade?" My voice timid, "What do you want?"

"I want to live and see where it takes me. I want to have someone special to share everything with. I want to be creative. I want passion. I don't have a plan to get married, have 2.4 kids and live behind a white picket fence. I want my life to show me what's in store for me, not make a plan and execute it." He stopped. "It's not that I don't want to get married or I don't want any kids. I'm letting it happen and not forcing it."

Maybe he's got this right. Plan on calling in sick and you end up sick, not enjoying the day with a hot photographer. I'm supposed to trust the world to send me down the right path? Keep me fed, clothed and sheltered? I'd probably start having anxiety attacks. I start sweating and my tummy rolls. "I need to go rest."

"Do you need anything?"

"I need to sleep."

"Liv, you don't need to be perfect. Being you is better than being perfect."

"Everyone doesn't share your opinion."

"They don't have to. Get some rest and we will talk later. Relax, okay?"

"Okay, bye." I hang up, but I don't rest like I should. I can't stop replaying what he said in my head. I don't have a problem with his philosophy on life. I want to do more things I like to do, more things for me.

I have books I haven't read and I thumb through my e-reader until I find one I want to read. I read for a couple hours, before I rest and wake up in the middle of the night to pick the book up where I left off. I go back to sleep when the sun is coming up.

When I finally wake up at about 11am on Wednesday morning, my phone is blowing up. I have a missed call from Kade from earlier in the morning and texts.

Kade - Are you still up?

Kade - Call me when you wake up. I'll be up late.

Kade - I'm going to bed. Call me anyway. I want to know you're okay.

Kade - I hope you aren't getting worse.

Mom - Hope you're feeling better. Please check with me sometime today.

Kade - Good Morning

Kade - I'm officially worried about you

Kade - I need to know what you want for breakfast. Still on strictly toast or maybe stepping up to some pancakes or eggs?

Kade - I get it. I'll leave you alone.

What just happened? The sound is off on my phone and I didn't check it before I went to sleep or when I woke up. I always check my phone. I wonder if it's a sign of doing something for me. I don't want him to leave me alone.

To Kade - Good Morning

To Kade - I was reading and didn't check my phone

To Kade - Didn't mean to make you worry. Sorry.

Kade - :)

Kade - What were you reading?

To Kade - A novel on my e-reader... best beach read of the year from like 3 years ago.

Kade - It's getting late for breakfast. What can I bring you for lunch?

To Kade - You don't need to bring anything. I'll be fine.

Kade - I'll be happier if I bring you something.

To Kade - I'll be fine. Going to nuke some soup.

Kade - You can tell me to leave you alone.

Kade - I'll understand. Sooner is better.

To Kade - I'm looking forward to our date on Friday :)

Kade - :) Me too.

I get out of bed and put my soup in the microwave. I call Mom while I wait, but she doesn't answer and I leave her a message letting her know I'm feeling better. I slurp up every last drop of soup and get cleaned up. I stink and I need to shower. I need to change my bedding and do laundry. I want to finish reading my book. I can have it all.

I call my supervisor to make sure she got my message and let her know I would be out tomorrow, but I should be back on Friday. She told me not to push it and not to bring whatever I'd gotten into the office, it sounded like take the rest of the week off to me.

I strip my bed and put the clean bedding on it. My favorite sheets, soft brushed T-shirt material printed with stripes like a rainbow. I take a break and sit in my comfy chair to read for a bit. A couple hours later, I take a long shower. The warm water beating on my skin is refreshing and seems to be washing away everything ill. I wash my hair and tie it up in a knot while I use my tropical shower gel with the little beads in it, coarse and slightly rough, wonderful texture rubbing on my skin. I usually don't take the time for it in the morning. I'm going to work, nothing special. I should use it everyday if for no other reason than it makes me happy to imagine a tropical place. The fact it feels good and leaves my skin glowing is a bonus. I close my eyes while I stand under the water and let it rinse away the soap, and I'm absorbed by Kade. We're in an outdoor shower together somewhere tropical like a rainforest. His wet hair pushed back out of his eyes and droplets of water on his eyelashes, his focus on me with nothing in the way. One of the few times he doesn't have a camera in his hands. His hands are on me and we're laughing. The way his body moves against me tells me he wants me, but he does nothing more than hold me and kiss me on the cheek, chaste at the corner of my lips. He wants more. There's buzzing energy coming off his body as he makes himself pull away. I'm hot and bothered. I want him and I want him now. It's not sane and it's not the way these things are supposed to go. You have to go on at least three dates before you give it up, and with me I've always stuck to at least three weeks, if not the three months rule. I guess those are expectations, too. I'm not doing what's expected anymore, I'm doing what I want. Shit. I can't do what I want, when what I want, wants to go slow. The irony is not lost on me. Kade told me to live, do things I want to do and be happy. I guess he didn't count on the thing I want to *do* most being him.

I dry off and pull on a pair of cut off sweats, and my old, over-worn James Blunt concert shirt. I plant myself in my chair and go back to reading.

CHAPTER 5

S tartled by knocking on my door, I check the time and it had gotten away from me, almost 9pm. I've been lost in reading, like when I was a kid. I'd find a quiet, secluded place, like the tree house in the backyard, or the top of the rocket slide at the park, or simply the corner of my room like I am right now, and read until someone stopped me. I remember one 4th of July when the whole family got together and they couldn't find me, I was in the corner of the dining room under the table with a book. The knock came again. I call out, "Who is it?" from my bedroom as I determine if I'm going to answer and need to find my robe.

"Kade. Are you okay?"

"I'm fine." I call back through the door and fantasize about what could happen if I invite him in.

"You weren't responding and I had to check on you. I have a pizza we can share."

"Are you sure you want to come in?" Replaying what I want to happen in my head and trying to focus.

"I don't think I'll get sick." So not at all what I was asking.

I laugh to myself, "One second." I run around my apartment

and find something acceptable to change into. There's no way I answer the door braless. I cuff my cutoffs, put on a bra and pull a cute T-shirt without holes in it out of my dresser, quickly pulling it over my head and deciding my hair still tied up in a knot on my head will have to be good enough. I open the door, "Hi. Come on in." I swing my arm out gesturing for him to enter when what I want to do is reach up around his neck and kiss him while I press my body against his.

He laughs while he looks at me and it's disturbing, "Why are you laughing at me? Do I look that bad? I'm sick you know."

"I don't think you're the kind of sick that's contagious. I also don't think you usually wear your shirt with the v-neck in the back."

Damn it. "I was changing quick. I didn't want to make you wait for me."

"You always look good, you didn't need to change for me." I smile at the sentiment. I had to change for me because I didn't want him to see me all grubby. I excuse myself and fix my shirt.

I return to find him sitting on my couch with the pizza on the coffee table. I grab a couple sodas from the refrigerator and sit down next to him. Not skipping a beat, I sit as close to him as possible, leaning against him and reaching my hand up around his neck to play with his hair. Seriously? What has gotten into me? Is this the result of a decade long crush? Am I so horny I can't control myself? Curious about the electrical current that shoots through me when he touches me? I'm guessing the answers are yes, yes, and yes.

He leans in and kisses my cheek, then reaches for the pizza to separate the slices. "Have you been sleeping all day? You look like you're feeling better."

"No, I took a short nap, but mostly I've been reading."

"We get dependent on our phones and don't put them down,

it's a good break when you can ignore it. Are you going back to work tomorrow?"

"No, I already called in. I'm off for the rest of the week."

"Don't feel well enough yet?"

"I want to stay home and read. Do something for me. I have weeks of sick time."

"I've created a monster," he laughs. "Maybe you should turn your phone sound on, in case of emergency. I'm pretty sure you haven't checked it in the last eight hours."

I glare at him and get up to go find my phone. Not only have I not used my phone, it's missing. I wander into my bedroom, it must be in there. Kade follows me, stopping at the doorway like there's some kind of invisible barrier he can't pass through. I turn, gazing at him, "Yeah, I wouldn't come in here if I were you either. I'm not sure it's safe for you in my living room." Maybe the problem is my filter. Could it be, I've been set at extreme constraint for too long?

The expression on his face is priceless.

I sit down on my bed, lean back on my hands and pat the bed. "Come over and have a seat."

His face tells me he's torn and truly all I'm doing is tormenting him, though I would put out for him in a second. He wants me and he wants to take it slow. Taking it slow might kill me.

A light flashes in the side of my comfy chair and it's my phone. I reach for it and I have texts.

"You can forget about those. I'm here now." Something clicks in my head, he's here now. He's at my place for the first time. Suddenly I'm an animal at the zoo being observed in my natural habitat, sitting on my bed in my white walled room, with my rainbow sheets, my turquoise comfy chair, and my electronics strewn around the room. I sit and read my texts, he won't come any closer to me and my bed.

Kade - Hi :)

Kade - Give me a call when you wake up

Kade - Hope you're feeling better

Mom - Sorry I missed your call. Happy you're feeling better.

Mom - You know I'm here if you need me.

Kade - You worry me when you don't respond

Kade - I don't want to play games with you

Kade - I like you, Liv. I think about you all the time.

Kade - I need to really know you and know it's real

Mark - You're not a bitch

Mark - I don't know why I said that

Kade - I had a crush on you in high school, maybe I have ever since.

Kade - You could break me

Kade - I need to know you're okay

Kade - I'll be by soon

Kade - What kind of pizza do you like?

I quickly glance at Kade, take my phone off silent, and...

To Kade - I've had a crush on you since high school, too.

To Kade - I know you have the power to break me

He's smiling at me and I can see he wants to say something, but isn't.

To Kade - I think kissing me would give you all the answers
you're looking for
To Kade - I want to feel your lips on mine
Kade - I want to kiss you
Kade - I want to do other things
To Kade - Are you thinking you should leave?
Kade - Yes, but I don't want to
To Kade - I think you should stay

"Let's go finish the pizza. Maybe we can find a movie to watch or something, give you a chance to relax and let me take care of you." Kade stops short, realizing what he had said. He reaches his hand out to me and I take it, allowing him to lead me back to the living room. Apparently, he thinks the living room is safer.

We sit together munching pizza and channel surfing until we find an old sitcom marathon. He's more relaxed now and has his arm around me. Everything right, he presses his lips to my cheek. He leans his head against the top of mine, pulling my head over to lean on his shoulder.

It's almost 2am when my phone starts going off, but I don't notice until there's movement. I open my eyes to find I fell asleep with my head in Kade's lap. He pulled the blanket I keep over the back of the couch down over me and had made himself comfortable with my throw pillows.

"Sorry, baby. I didn't mean to wake you up." His voice soft and low.

I stay where I am, not wanting to give up my position, "What's wrong?"

"Your phone is going crazy."

"Ignore it. You're here."

He reaches for it and hands it to me. "Who's Mark? I thought you said it's only me now."

"It is only you. Mark is the guy I was dating."

"He must still think he's dating you."

"He's an idiot." I look at the texts.

Mark - Just drove by your place and your lights are still on

Mark - How about a visit?

Mark - What are you wearing right now?

Mark - Babe, I miss you.

To Mark - I'm busy

To Mark - I already have a visitor

To Mark - Go away

Mark - You have another guy up there?

Mark - You just dumped me and you already have new dick

To Mark - Yes

To Mark - I'm feeling much better by the way, thanks for asking.

To Mark - We're done and I don't want to talk to you, or anything else.

To Mark - I thought I was clear last time

I hand my phone to Kade, so he would set it over on the table and not worry that I'm hiding something. "Anything you want to tell me?" He asks as he takes my phone.

"Nothing that matters. Only you matter. I have no other guys and no interest in any other guys."

"That's quite a statement."

"It's true, and it's killing me."

"What?"

I hide my face from him, "I'm going to spontaneously combust if I don't get to have you soon. Fuck. I'm such a guy."

I hear laughing. Kade is actually laughing. "Stop it!" I smack his arm where I can reach. I'm mad at Mark for waking us up. I can't believe I fell asleep on Kade, but waking up there is perfect and I want to do it again.

"I guess I should go home."

"You should stay. Having you here with me helped me sleep." It's true, don't judge me.

"That's dangerous, Liv. Where would we sleep?"

"We can sleep on the couch, like we already were or you can sleep in my bed with me. Whichever you prefer and I promise to keep my clothes on."

"It's a bad idea, but I want you to get some sleep. Let's go, time for you to go to bed."

Searching him doe-eyed, "Are you going with me?"

He releases an exasperated sigh, "Yes."

I climb in bed and pull the sheet up over me. I point out where the bathroom is and tell him to make himself at home. I watch Kade as he toes his shoes off and sits down on the foot of my bed. There must be something wrong with me. The weight of him sitting on the foot of my bed sends flutters through my happy place. He yanks his shirt off, revealing his bare chest and there's no other way to say it. I'm wet. His chest isn't perfect, but defined enough to show he has pecks and his torso has outlines of a four pack, he isn't cut. I continue to watch the show, halfway wanting to yell "take it off!" like at the strip club. I consider what else might come off and figure he will probably sleep in his jeans. "I can't sleep in my jeans. Are you okay with me sleeping in my boxer briefs? Maybe you have some sweats I can borrow or something?"

I most certainly do have sweats he can borrow, "You're fine in your boxer briefs. I don't mind. Too warm for sweats anyway." Hey, a girl can hope.

He turns the light off and stands facing away from me while he takes his jeans off, folding his clothes neatly and setting them in my chair. He sits on the side of the bed and lifts his legs up, lying on top of the sheet. He leans over me and kisses my left eyelid, then my right, then each of my cheeks three times each like he's making sure he doesn't miss a spot, then across my forehead, down the bridge of my nose, and my chin. He only misses one place and my body is buzzing from the sweet kisses he has planted all over my face. "Goodnight, Liv." He presses a chaste kiss to each corner of my mouth and lays down next to me. He reaches for me and pulls me against him, spooning me with his arms around me snug, and his heart beating at my back. "I'm glad you asked me to stay. This is what I need. You're what I need." There's silence and when I wake up during the night, he's still here holding me.

I wake up warmer than usual and remember Kade is with me. He's on his back with his arm holding me to him. My head is resting on his shoulder, with my hand on his bare chest, our legs entangled at our feet and his lips pressed to my forehead. I'm happy. I slept well. My illness has faded away. Kade is here. I take a deep breath, relaxing and loving him in my bed with me, comfortable and cuddling his bare chest.

"Can I make you coffee or breakfast or something? When do you have work?"

He kisses my forehead. "I'm calling in sick, and spending the day with you."

My heart drops and if I hadn't started to fall already, if I wasn't already in trouble, it would be official now. I smile and giggle uncontrollably.

"I like that sound. I like my girl to be happy. Let's stay like this a little longer."

Who am I to argue? I snuggle into him, give his shoulder a kiss and close my eyes. I ignore his morning wood because I don't want to make him uncomfortable. I hope he stays over again. I couldn't help notice how substantial he is. I bet he usually sleeps in the nude, he obviously wants to be released. It's all I can do not to comment on it and tell him it would be okay for him to sleep naked.

He places his finger under my chin and lifts until his lips are on mine. My eyes close of their own will when his warm, soft lips are held against mine for a few seconds and released. Chaste, yet my heart is beating like I ran a marathon. "Sorry, I shouldn't have done that. It's not really appropriate to kiss you for the first time when I'm mostly naked in your bed. I might as well be taking advantage of you in your sleepy state."

"You can't take advantage of someone who's willing." I splay my hand on his chest and slowly move it down to his abs, exploring him while I kiss his chest, then his collarbone and his neck. My breath is heavy, "We should get up now."

He pulls me over him, laying me on his chest and holding me tight. He's fighting with himself, his need. He takes my hands in his, so I can sit up and feel his impressive bulge under my heat. I can't help myself, I grind against him and release a needy whimper. He sits up immediately and presses his lips to mine again. I've lost control and lick his lips, asking him to open for me and deepen the kiss. He leans his mouth to my ear and reaches his arms around my waist. "You know I want you. Fuck, Liv, you're grinding against how much I want you. I want to kiss and lick every part of you. I want to know it's more than want. I need to know we're both in this." He lifts me up and gets out of bed, taking me with him. He sets me down, leaving me standing next to him. "Don't you want the same thing?"

I contemplate for a minute, because I do want the same thing. The problem is I also want to fuck his brains out right now. "Yes. Okay, I'll try to not want you so much," I giggle and he gives me a funny chastising look, "I need to tell you one thing before I attempt good behavior."

"What?"

"I'm so wet right now, I need to go shower. That's all."

"That's all?"

"Yeah, unless you want to find out how wet I am. Wet for you, that is."

"Are you done now?"

"Good behavior starts now."

He grabs me around the waist and lifts me up over his head, brushing his lips across my crotch. He groans as he sets me down. "One more thing I have to taste, more now that I know you smell so sweet." His hands on my waist move down my hips and I can see his focus shift as his hands move to my thighs. He sits on the edge of my bed, watching me and not moving. I take his hand in mine and cup my sex with it. I shouldn't have, but he takes control and doesn't complain. He rubs his hand against me and I want more, my hips buck. "You need to get off. Too wound up for your own good. No way you can be on good behavior. I'll leave and let you handle business. We can meet at the diner."

"You don't need to leave. I can wait for you." Then under my breath, "I don't do that."

"Nobody has been taking care of you. When you're mine, you'll always be taken care of. I promise you. I bet you've never really experienced sex the way it's supposed to be. Tell me what you feel when you come." I look at him to see he's serious. "It's okay, I need to know. I don't want to scare you or hurt you. I want you to enjoy it. I want you to want more."

"It's sliding in and out of me, sometimes a little harder and getting faster."

He splays his hand on my back and his other hand at my wet sex, "This isn't for me. I'm helping you. I need you to be able to wait with me. Focus on what you're telling me, about the details and your words. Don't think about me."

His hand slides up my shorts and moves my panties to the side. A finger travels along my heat, finding my wetness and sliding into exactly the right place. "Oh, it pushed in and pulled out, over and over. There's a little friction and my body might get tense, try to stiffen. The strokes would get faster and harder, only a few harder strokes then there would be pulsating with bodies mashed together." His finger is stroking into me and I need it bad.

"Keep going, baby. Tell me how it finishes."

"That's everything."

"No, that's not everything. Relax, baby." He turns me and lays me down on the bed. "I'm not taking anything off you, it's not the time. I don't get to have anything until it's us and I get to have you around me, okay, Liv?"

"I trust you to do whatever you want."

"Not helping, Liv."

"Okay. Don't take my clothes off, just get me off."

"This is going to be quick, not like when it's us. When it's us, you will never want anyone else again. Remember that, Liv." He slides his finger in and out, his fingers on his artistic hands with his great dexterity, suddenly I feel fuller and the strokes become faster, a little harder. This is nothing like what I experienced with Mark or anyone before him. "Good girl, I know you're feeling it, it's getting closer." My body moves on his fingers, out of my control and noises come from me I've never made before. His thumb travels up my seam and caresses me in a very sensitive area, circling lightly at first, then rubbing against it harder with his strokes into me and I'm screaming out in pleasure. My muscles clench hard around his fingers and convulse. He doesn't stop stroking me. He keeps his actions going and slows slightly. "Are you okay?"

"Uh-huh."

"I want to cheat and have something for myself. Something to help me wait."

I should tell him no and help the cause, "You said it's not you. It was just getting me off. What do you want?"

"I want to taste you."

"Lick your fingers."

He strokes into me hard a couple times, selfishly for himself before pulling out. I don't watch, but I hear him suck on his fingers as he pulls them out of his mouth. "I knew it. Sweet. So sweet. I'll be taking care of you all the time and I promise to make sure you're ready for me before you get to have all of me. I can't wait for you to experience us together."

I should be embarrassed, but I'm not. I giggle, "I'm going to jump in the shower real quick and change, okay? Can we walk to the park?"

"Sounds perfect. Liv?"

"Yeah?"

"You're special to me. I said it wasn't me, but I still want you to know I haven't been with a woman since my first trip to Europe. It's been over five years. You make me want to do things I didn't imagine ever happening again."

I smile, but I feel the pressure on the inside to live up to his expectations. As much as I'm not making choices based on what's expected, I want to be what Kade needs. I reach my arms around his neck and hug him tight, whispering, "You're special to me, too. I'm not sure anyone else ever really mattered." I kiss his cheek and dash to the shower.

CHAPTER 6

We walk to the old downtown holding hands. I love the way he immediately grasps my hand entangling our fingers, occasionally rubbing his thumb across my hand. My mind wanders to what he's thinking about when he does that. If it's nothing or maybe a nervous action? Is he simply enjoying the silkiness of my skin? Is he remembering what he did with his hands earlier? We stop at his office and he changes into the extra clothes he has stashed there. I'm surprised to see him in cargo shorts and an old White Stripes concert T-shirt, which has to work to make it around his shoulders. It's sexy, how his shorts ride low and his shirt almost meets them. I didn't notice his happy trail last night. He's going commando. His boxer briefs came up higher than the shorts. Damn! He's going commando. He grabs a camera out of his cabinet and brings it with him.

"You do everything today and I'm going to follow you," he says with a devious expression on his face and a camera in his hand.

"I'm sorry, what?" I glare at him like he's off his rocker.

"When we walk into the coffee shop, you take the lead and order for both of us. You do all the interacting, so I can watch and photograph it. I want to show you what I see and the difference when it's through my lens."

"Okay, I'll play your game." Coffee is the first thing on my mind. The camera didn't keep him from holding my hand until he needed distance or an angle he couldn't get while tethered to me. I walk up to the counter and all I can focus on is donuts.

"What can I get for you today, ma'am?" The young girl behind the counter addresses me like I'm old.

I stare at her and a sneer starts across my lips. Ideas cross through my mind of ordering the most complicated coffee drink of all time and sending it back, telling her it's wrong just because I can, but I don't do it. "A large mocha and a large caramel latte. Oooh, and I need donuts. Give me that raised glazed donut with the little hole in the middle, the cinnamon twist bar, a couple glazed holes and, look at that, you have holes with nuts! I need four of those. That should do." I turn to Kade and his cheeks are red, but he's shooting away. I pay for our breakfast and we take it to go, choosing to sit in the park and enjoy our sick day.

We walk the couple blocks to the park and find a bench under a full-canopied shade tree near the pathway. It's a warm day, but the shade and the light breeze make it bearable. We joke about the donuts and inhale every last bite of them. Nut coated holes are my new favorite. We walk the pathway through the park hand in hand, simply enjoying being together. Kade takes photos as we meander the pathway and when we get to the playground, he stops. His eyes travel my face and he points at the swings, "Go." I'm an adult and I consider stating that fact for less than half a second before I take off for the swings at full speed. Isn't the point of living enjoying yourself and spending time with the people you love? Love is an interesting word. There's no need to adult today. I erase everything from my mind and I survey the park, grateful for the empty playground. I sit in the middle swing and walk as far backwards as I can, hop up into the swing and kick forward while I hang onto the chains. I pull my feet back as I swing back and kick forward again, repeating the process until I'm flying high. The breeze as it brushes passed my face and blows my hair around is invigorating and gives me freedom to enjoy life. I'm laughing and screaming like a child as I swing. I've been happier the last few days, even home sick, than I can ever remember being. Kade jumps into the seat next to me and catches up with me quickly, each of us reaching for the sky with each kick. He reaches for my hand while we're swinging and we keep pace with each other, one of the sweetest things ever. He's watching me, smiling, truly happy, and I am, too.

We spend most of the day in the park, visiting the swings a handful of times. We fed the ducks and ran from a goose that wanted my cheese puffs. We climbed the kid's fort and sat on top of the monkey bars. At sunset, he led me back to the swings and I guessed it had something to do with the lighting. He shot photos all day and the light in his eyes as sunset approached was evident. He told me which swing to use, which direction to face, and talked the whole time, drawing different expressions to my face.

At the end of the day I'm tired and tomorrow is Friday, date night and my last sick day. I want to spend the whole time with Kade, and I want to finish reading my book.

We stop at the diner and I take control, ordering take out without asking what he wants. I order chili cheese fries, a cheeseburger and two shakes. When the order is ready, I pick it up and start walking back to my place. He doesn't question me, he goes along with me seamlessly. Sitting with him and sharing dinner two nights in a row, we've been together for nineteen hours and I don't want him to leave. I inspect him closely, learning the lines of his face while he sits at the table with me and my heart sinks at the thought of him leaving.

He makes a squinched face and focuses on me, "What's wrong?"

"Are you staying with me tonight or going home?"

"Which answer makes you smile and gets rid of the frown you have on?"

"Staying with me."

"I'm staying here with you tonight, but I need to run home to get clothes and I need to get up and leave in the morning. I have work to do and things to prep for our date."

I smile, "Okay." He left after a little bit. I napped while he was gone and he woke me when he texted because I didn't answer the door.

Kade - I'm at your door
To Kade - :)
To Kade - I was asleep
Kade - I can go home and let you rest
To Kade - No, I want you here.
Kade - Are you going to let me in?

I didn't want to get up.

To Kade - Use the key hiding on top of the porch lamp
Kade - Seriously? Not a safe hiding place.

The door latch clicks and the floor creaks at Kade's footsteps.

"I'm in the bedroom. Nothing crazy, just napping," I giggle at myself for having to justify. He's back freshly showered, wearing clean clothes and with his duffle bag in hand. He sets his bag on the floor, toes off his shoes and climbs into bed with me without missing a beat.

"Hi," he wraps his arms around me and hugs me.

"Last night you didn't want to enter my bedroom and tonight you didn't think twice about climbing into my bed. Is that a sign of progress or a sign I'm easy?" I giggle.

"Progress. You're not easy." His voice thick, "It's different between us." He leans over me like he had the night before and kisses me a bunch of times all over my face, but in the end he didn't stop at the corners of my mouth—he presses his lips to mine and holds them there. He brings his hands to my face and holds it. He pulls back and looks at me, his smile spreads across his face. He brings his mouth back to mine and it's different this time, he nibbles at my lips, kisses each of my lips and opens his mouth, sliding his tongue against mine in a sensual dance. This is the kiss I've been waiting for. It shoots through me, sending tingles to every nerve in my body. He wants me, and he wants more as he moves over me, resting his weight on me while he kisses me and holds me. At the brush of his lips and open mouth, the butterflies in my gut turn to hummingbirds and my desire is in charge. His electrical current travels to my farthest extremities and the only thing that exists is Kade. My hands roam his body uncontrolled. I need every piece of him I can reach. I need his hands on me exploring my body. He pulls away and comes back again, kissing me sweetly, tenderly, open-mouthed repeatedly. He stops and gazes into my eyes. My reflection shining back at me, my own eyes showing me the truth I haven't admitted to myself yet. We're both overcome at the same time and he controls it, kissing me sweetly and pulling away while he holds me in his arms.

"Liv, remember I went to work when you wake up in the morning. It's only you and me. I need you, baby. Goodnight." His arms snug around me, protecting me while he holds me on his chest. His nose buried in my hair and his lips pressed to my forehead as we fall asleep.

I sleep better in his arms than I ever have. I wake up late in the morning alone and have a text waiting for me.

Kade - Good morning

Kade - I'm at my office working and plan to pick you up about 5pm

Kade - Sweats and a hoodie to pull on over shorts would be appropriate

Kade - This is not a dress up date

Kade - Besides, you're beautiful no matter what. <3

To Kade - Good morning :)

Kade - I used your extra house key to lock your door and I took it with me. You need a better hiding place for it. It wasn't in a safe place.

To Kade - Keep it :)

Kade - :) :) :)

Kade - Are you sure?

To Kade - I'm already yours. You should have my key, too.

I stay in bed, surrounded by the sent of Kade while I finish reading my book. I set my e-reader on my night table and find tears running down my face. I don't want the story to be over. I need to know what happens next. Does he leave again? Is he back for good? Does he love her? This is how it used to be. I'd get completely sucked in and forget the world around me. I'd escape. I need more of this. Maybe if I escaped more, the world would be easier and I wouldn't need a change. When I'm with Kade, I don't want to escape.

I putz around my apartment for the rest of the afternoon, getting my laundry caught up and trying not to get nervous about my date. I don't know why I'd be nervous. He has spent the night twice. I've spent most of the last two days with him. I love the way he holds me, and his mouth, his lips; when he kisses me I don't need anything else.

I pack my tote bag with sweatpants, leggings, a hoodie, T-shirt, and chocolate for survivals sake. I get ready early and sit down with my e-reader to find my next read.

CHAPTER 7

Kade - I'll be there early. I want to show you some photos
before we go.

To Kade - I'm ready whenever you get here

Kade - :)

About 4:30 there's someone climbing up my stairs and a
knock on my door. "Let yourself in," I call out.

"The door is locked and the extra key is gone." The voice isn't
Kade's. I check the peephole as discreetly as I can, but I recognized the voice when it boomed through my apartment. Mark is
at my door.

I yell back through the door, "I wasn't expecting you."

"Let me in."

"No."

"I need to talk to you."

"We don't have anything to talk about."

He bangs on my door. "Olivia! Open the door," he says with a
slur in his speech.

"We're done. Go sleep it off, asshole!"

"I'm not done." He tries to open my door and I make sure both deadbolts are secured.

"Go home. I'm taking my bat to your head if you come through my door."

"Bullshit. You don't own a bat."

"Proof you never paid attention to me you selfish jerk."

"Olivia! I love you, babe. Please stay with me. Move in with me. I miss you."

I consider going into my bedroom locking the door and putting my headphones on until he goes away, but it's getting close to 5pm.

To Kade - You might want to wait a few minutes until the scene clears.

To Kade - Ex is at my door and I think he's drunk.

To Kade - Sorry

Kade - I'm sitting across the street watching

Kade - Does he know you played softball in high school?

Kade - I wouldn't want to piss you off when you have a bat

"Olivia! Did you hear me? I love you."

"I don't love you and I never have."

"I know you don't mean that."

"Go away and don't come back!"

He shakes my door violently and the window rattles. "You know the truth."

"The truth is I want nothing to do with you. Get it through your thick skull."

He shoulders my door, trying to break it down and another voice in the background has my heart racing. "She told you to leave. You should do that now." I peek out the window and Kade is yelling up at him from the bottom of the stairs.

"Mind your own business, dude."

"Liv is my girl, not yours."

Kade got Mark's attention. "I don't know who the fuck you are, but Olivia only dates me."

I yell through the door, "How many times do I have to dump you for you to understand we're over! I'm not dating you anymore. Go to your poker game. Maybe one of the guys there will want to screw you."

Kade laughs out and Mark starts down the stairs after him. I shoulder my tote bag, grab my bat and open my door. I'm ready to knock his block off. Mark throws a punch at Kade, but he ducks. "Kade!" I scream out like he's not right there observing this all happen firsthand. It happens so quickly, I see Mark go flying over Kade's shoulder and hit the ground. I swear his landing almost had a comical bounce.

"Come on, Liv. Let's get out of here." I lock the door behind me and run down the stairs.

Mark rolls to his side and lies there. I stop and stand a couple feet away from him tapping my bat on the ground. "I was hoping I'd get to use my bat."

"We'll go to the batting cages tomorrow." Kade gestures for me to go to him and I run to his side, his arm instantly wraps around me. He leads me to a cool rag-top Volkswagen Bus and we take off quickly.

"Sorry about that." I reach over and touch his leg while he's driving.

He puts his hand on mine and holds it there unless he has to shift. "I'm glad I was there. If he shows up drunk again, the first thing you should do is let me know. You shouldn't have to deal with him by yourself."

"You saw my bat, right?" my adrenaline still flowing.

"Yes, and I know you can use it. I know you can take care of yourself, but I want to keep you safe."

I smile at how he wants to take care of me and wonder what

has gotten into me when my insides go all mushy. "So, where are we going?" The curtain is pulled dividing the front seats from the back of the bus and I reach to peek behind it.

"Don't peek. It's part of the date. I reserved us a spot up at Celestial Park."

"Stargazing?"

"Eventually, too cheesy? I've always wanted to go and it might be romantic," he glances toward me, the first time I've ever seen him unsure about anything.

"I love the adventure and getting to be with you." I need to watch the L word closely, it seems to be making it's way into my sentences more easily lately. He drives us up a mountain road surrounded by tall pine trees and stops at the Celestial Outpost. We walk in, he goes to the counter to check in and get our assigned spot while I wander about perusing the funny shirts and swag. I didn't know there were so many ways to make jokes about the moon and mooning people. Kade finds me and leads me back to the bus. He drives us into the park and finds our spot. It's probably the highest spot in the campground, the best for stargazing.

CHAPTER 8

"I hope you don't mind, I brought cameras with me. I have camera mounts installed on the top of the bus and this would be a great opportunity to set up some automatic shots, some time lapse. The sun setting over the mountains is gorgeous. I have dinner and other plans for us this evening. We have all night to ourselves. We can turn our phones off and be alone together." He leans in, kissing me square on the lips. He pulls back and smiles, waiting for a reaction.

"I don't expect you to go anywhere without your camera. Everything, everywhere is an opportunity." I grab my phone and call Mom. Kade watches me funny as I dial my phone.

"Hey, Livi, how are you?"

"Hi, Mom. I took the whole week off and I'm completely better. I needed time to relax."

"I'm glad to hear it."

"Anyway, I'm calling you real quick to let you know I'm camping at Celestial Park tonight with Kade. I'm turning my phone off and I'll message you in the morning."

"The photographer?"

"Yeah, we've been hanging out all week and this is our first real date."

"I can hear in your voice that you'll have a great time and you're well taken care of. Be safe, Livi, and call if you need me. Thanks for letting me know you're going off the grid for the night."

"Bye, Mom." I hang up and Kade smiles at me.

"Did you check in with your Mom and tell her we're dating?"

"I guess I did. I don't want her to worry because I'm all yours tonight." I turn off my phone and drop it in my tote bag.

"Commitment, I like it." He turns his phone off and tosses it in the glove box. "Ready?"

I turn to him unsure, "For what?" He opens all the curtains in the bus, exposing all the windows and pulling the rag-top open. There's a bench across the back covered in Hawaiian print with a bunch of throw pillows. He flips open a convertible table in the middle of the space and points out the ice chest with drinks and snacks in it. He opens a picnic basket that's filled to the brim, packed by the deli with enough food for six and turns some soft music on low.

"What do you think?"

"It's cool," I grin happily.

"Walk up to the point there with me for sunset?" He watches me, waiting for my response, and extends his hand. We lean on a big rock together watching the sky change colors as it goes from light blue to yellow to purple and the sun disappears behind the pines. He takes a few photos of the sun and a few of me with the sunset behind me. "You're beautiful, Liv. I need to show you the photos."

When the sun was gone, we got comfortable in the back of the bus and Kade spread photos out all over the table. They were all me. I'm happy in every single one. There are close-ups, full body shots, black and whites, basically everything I did yesterday was caught on film—almost. "This one is..." He points to a black and white close-up of me on the swings, laughing with my hair flying everywhere, "I love it. I also love this one, but for a whole different reason." He shows me one of me eating donuts, a donut hole coated in nuts to be specific, and I was playing it up. The next one he shows me was on the swings again, but this one was full color with the sunset behind me and showed the whole swings structure. It depicts me as almost a shadow or silhouette, with the sunlight bouncing off the metal of the swings as well as the rays shining through my hair as it flies through the air. "What do you think?"

"They're technically superb, but the woman in these photos is free and happy, loving life." I consider the effect he's had on me the last few days, how his presence makes my body flutter. Maybe I do look like that. Maybe he's bringing my happy back.

"It's exactly how you look, the camera doesn't lie. It's how you always look to me."

He closes the side door and makes sure all the van doors are locked Then he pulls the curtains closed over the side windows and the divider from the front seats. He hits a button and little lights sparkle along the top of the curtain all the way around the bus. "The best time for shooting stars tonight starts after midnight. We have time to eat dinner and hang out together. We can put the table away and pull the bed out, so we can lie here together and watch for shooting stars or whatever you want." I stare at him like he's dinner and he must have caught the *sex please* in my eyes. "Okay, almost anything you want." He pulls me close and kisses me again, slowly cherishing my lips. "I promise lots of kissing tonight and I will have you in my arms at every possible moment. The first time is special and it needs to be in the privacy of our own bedroom, where we can take all night long and I can show you how I feel about you."

"How do you feel about me?"

"Scared of what you make me want and how you make me feel. You're all I think about and I keep wanting to do things for you. I want to take care of you."

I giggle, "I felt silly when I was home alone this afternoon because I missed you." I blush and my cheeks get warm.

"Don't. I missed you, too." He leans his forehead to mine and pulls my body against his. "I wanted to kill that guy for being a jerk to you."

"You told him I'm your girl."

"Yeah, I did. It's what I want. I don't want to date you. I want you to be my girl and I don't want you seeing any other men. I can't believe I'm in this place again, completely into a woman after such a short time. I can't help myself." He runs his fingers through his hair, pulling it back tight.

I press my finger to his cheek and turn his face to mine. "It doesn't make any sense, but I'm right here with you. Maybe it's been a long time, we've known each other since high school."

"I told myself to take it slow and learn everything about you. Every time I said anything to you about taking it slow and waiting, I was telling myself."

I gaze into his eyes trying to read him and say the right words, "I don't want to be with anyone, but you." I kiss him, claiming him as mine and leaving no question about it.

"Do you want to stay at my place with me for the rest of the weekend?"

"Yes, I want you with me every night."

"I travel some, but most nights I can make that happen," he stops and continues, "Unless, you want to travel with me."

"Sounds like fun. A grand adventure."

"Liv, you could be my grand adventure," his voice low and raspy as he says the words. I'm engulfed by his emotion. The honest truth rolling through me like a roller coaster I was excited to ride, but anxious about the loop. I've wanted him for so long. I need to have the courage to go after what I want. His eyes hold me with his gaze and he splays his fingers across my back, pulling me to him. His lips brush mine gently. He pulls back and inspects the floor without releasing me. I run my fingers through his hair and he brings his focus back to me, kissing me again and holding his lips to mine. Zips of electricity bounce between us. I bite his lower lip softly and he groans from a low inside place. My hands move to his chest, roaming as I explore his upper body. He draws a line of kisses from my mouth to my neck and whispers, "I love the way your hands feel on me." The sensation of his warm breath pulls a needy whimper from my lips and he presses open-mouthed kisses to my neck. My body reacts without me, stretching my neck back and arching into him. I want him to touch me. His hands move to my hips and his fingers dig in, like he wants something else and he's trying to keep them in control. His mouth travels back to mine, tenderly asking for admission he strokes his tongue into my mouth for a sexy slow dance and his hands drop to my ass, squeezing and pulling me closer to him. His large, artists hands on me, comforting and needy. The drawn out slow kiss has us both burning, hearts beating out of our chests and unable to breathe. I pull back trying to catch my breath and stare at him. He traces my lips with his finger, "I know, Liv, me, too." He holds me close and we smile at each other foolishly in silence.

Kade turns into the host and sets dinner out on the table. It's a smorgasbord of deli delights. There are containers of olives, pickles, salads, grapes, sandwiches sliced into bites, mac and cheese, cake and tiramisu. He grabs a couple bottled waters out of the cooler and I help him open all the containers while he gets the forks and napkins. We sit hip to hip with his arm around me and my hand on his knee, each of us left with one hand to fork and eat the feast of bites. We smile and laugh as we try every-thing, sharing from each other's fork and enjoying time together.

Kade turns the lights off and holds my hand. We lean back into the pillows and gaze out the roof at the stars. The vast darkness of the night sky, lit only by celestial bodies. It's quiet, calm, and so clear the sky looks like it's been sprinkled with diamond dust.

"There's Polaris," I point and remember which constellations I can find from the North Star.

"You know astronomy?"

"Only a little. Basic stuff. I like it, because it's always moving and yet somehow patterned over time."

"I challenge you."

"What's the game?"

"Back and forth identifying objects in the sky until we run out."

"What do I get when I win?"

"I like your confidence, but you have no idea what I know or don't know about it. Winner gets choice of dessert and gets to pick the side of the bed they want to sleep on."

"Deal. Your turn, I already identified Polaris."

"Big Dipper," he points it out drawing a line from the North Star.

"Little Dipper," I point, "Polaris is the end of the handle."

"Northern Cross," he points and outlines it in the air.

"Denab, it's the bright star of the Northern Cross."

"Lyra, the harp is straight down from the Northern Cross."

"Are you ready to give up yet?" I say challenging and look at him. "I'll understand and I'll share the dessert with you. No shame in admitting defeat before it goes too far."

He laughs, "Nope. You out already?"

I squint my eyes at him, "Cygnus, the swan, extend the arms of the Northern Cross out another star. I won't judge you if you want to give up now."

"Summer Triangle, Polaris, the bright star of Lyra and that extra bright star over there," he says pointing.

"The bright star of Lyra is called Vega and, for good measure, that extra bright star over there is Altair."

"Uh-oh, you're disqualified for showing off with two answers on one turn. Smarty pants."

"Changing the rules mid-game and to your advantage? Tsk, tsk." I laugh at the top of my lungs because I really don't care. I want to touch him and all I can think about ever since he said bed, is opening the bed.

Kade laughs with me and puts the table down, like he's reading my mind. "Move to the front seat for a minute, and I'll open the bed. It'll be an easier view straight up." I move as he asks and he throws the pillows at me one at a time, knowing I have nowhere to put them. He opens the bed and it takes up almost the whole back of the bus. He wraps it in a sheet he has that's made to fit it and I start throwing the pillows back at him before he's ready. He pulls a huge fluffy comforter out from behind where the bench had been and spreads it out on the bed. He reaches back there again and pulls out a couple big pillows. I crawl onto the bed, directly to him and knock him down flat on is back. I crawl right up him and lay on top of him, resting my head on his chest where I can feel his heartbeat.

"Okay, what are you doing?"

"Lying on you, it's comfortable and warm. Except..."

"Except what?"

"It would be better if you didn't have a shirt on." Shoes had been lost hours ago and it's not like I said *Take your pants off sailor!*

"Liv..."

"I like your chest."

"I'm sure I'd like your chest, too," he says with a chuckle.

"I can take my shirt off, too."

"Yes, I mean I understand it's a possibility." He runs his hand through his hair. "You know I want you. I don't want to rush this, us."

"What if it's not rushing it? What if we're wasting time we could be, um, closer?" I roll off of him and watch frustration take over his handsome features.

"You can't be logical about this. There's nothing logical about this."

"Tell me something I don't know, Kade. You think I have men over to spend the night in their underwear before I've dated them for a couple months, let alone before I've been on a single date with them? You think I can fall asleep with just anybody? You think I let anyone finger bang me? Do you think I've ever taken a sick day when I wasn't sick anymore? Do you think I've given my key to anyone else, ever? Am I just a horny girl that's easy and fun to play with? I can't help it when I'm with you and it's never been this way before. Nobody has ever had this effect on me. Damn it." I sit up and crawl to the front seats searching for my shoes and hiding my face from him.

"Stop! Liv, please."

I put my sweats on over my clothes and slip my sneakers on. Kade is rustling around in the bus. I turn to open my door and he's standing there gesturing for me to roll the window down. I pull the hood up over my head and drawstring the face closed, hiding from him in plain sight. I don't want him to find the tears streaming down my face. I don't roll down the window, I open the door into him and he allows it to open. I step out of the bus and he puts his arms around me, pulling me snug against him.

I pull away from his embrace and start walking. I have no idea where I'm going.

He keeps pace with me. "Where are we going?"

"I'm going for a walk."

"I'm going with you. It's not safe out here by yourself this late, it's dark and you don't have your phone."

I walk to the van and grab my bat with Kade following behind, then start to walk away. "You don't have a trail map. You don't know where you're going. It's not safe."

"I'm tired of making the safe choice and I don't need a babysitter."

"Get in the bus and I'll take you home if that's what you want."

"What I want is you! I want to feel the things I only feel when I'm with you, when you touch me, the electric spark that flashes between us when we kiss, the fluttering in my belly when you stand near me, the buzz that overtakes me when our tongues meet. I need to know what else there is between us. I need to know we're the whole package and we both feel it. It never mattered. Nothing ever mattered. I've been coasting through, not living. I want to feel things, experience things, and I want to do it with you. Damn it!" I turn and start to walk away, but he grabs me and presses me up against the van with his body. He rips my hood off my head and puts his mouth on mine, hot and needy, demanding. His cock hard between us.

He pulls back suddenly, "I didn't mean to make you cry. I never want to hurt you." His eyes searching mine.

"It's not your fault. Well, I guess it is, but you didn't hurt me —you make me feel. I don't want guys to see me be weak."

"Crying isn't weak and I'm not just a guy. At least, I hope I'm not just a guy." He continues to search my eyes, and I wish I could read his thoughts, find out what he wants "I want to drag you back to my cave like a caveman right now. Fuck. You make me nuts. I can't see straight." Kade loses it, picking me up and lifting my legs up around him while claiming my mouth. I have no choice but to wrap my legs around him, I can't reach the ground and, my god, why wouldn't I wrap my legs around this man? He takes control of everything. He opens the side door to the van and sets me down on the bed, immediately locking the door behind him and climbing in over me. He turns the music up and proceeds to take my shoes off. "You're not going anywhere. Fuck. I sound like a controlling asshole." I giggle uncontrollably. He stops and looks at me, "What? Now you're laughing at me? What's funny?"

"Nothing."

"Why are you laughing?"

"You want me," I say happily. "Will you take your shirt off now, please?"

"Fuck, yes." He pulls his shirt off and I sit straddling his lap while I get to know his chest, intimately, with my tongue.

CHAPTER 9

I wake up laying on Kade's bare chest, the morning light creeping in to find us wrapped up together in the fluffy comforter. His arms are around me with no sign of letting go, our legs entangled. He's still sleeping and I don't want to disturb him. I lie still enjoying his steady breathing, relaxing to his heartbeat. I have no idea what time it is and it doesn't matter. I close my eyes and go back to sleep.

I wake up when Kade reaches for the rag-top and pulls it closed as far as he can without getting up. He rolls toward me on his side, brings me into his chest and pulls the comforter up over our heads. "Let's stay like this awhile longer, okay, baby?"

"Mmm hmm." I slide my sweatpants off, wanting my bare legs against him and he pushes his pants off. "Mmmm, even better." I kiss his chest and snuggle in, somehow managing to keep my hands above his waist.

He kisses the top of my head, and runs his hand up and down my back. I want to take my shirt off, so I can feel his hands touch my skin, but I shouldn't push him. He finds the bottom edge of my shirt and skims his hand up my shirt, exploring my back and my waist. I whisper quietly, "You can take my shirt off. My bra covers more than most bikinis. If you want to. No pressure or anything."

He groans and curses, and my shirt comes off. His hands, his big warm hands hold me to him. Touching me, exploring me, wanting me. His thumb brushing back and forth over my waist while his fingers are splayed across my belly and back. Both his hands glide up my back to my head and tangle in my hair. He uses my hair to angle my mouth to him and he looks into my wide eyes, "Good morning." He smiles as he presses his lips to mine and I feel it everywhere. Everywhere. Instantly wet and breathing heavy, I moan under my breath. "You're not alone." He takes my hand and holds it on his morning wood. "We want you, too." Fuck me. He slips his tongue into my mouth and the burn continues. His arm wraps around my waist, holding me tightly to him. His mouth on mine and our tongues dancing together. His cock moving against my hand. I don't know what to do. I know what I want to do, but I don't want to go beyond the boundaries.

Go after what you want, Olivia. Quietly, "May I touch you?"

"Yes," his voice rough, "Please, Liv, touch me."

I carefully push his boxer briefs down and reach my lips back to his, pressing my lips to his and darting my tongue into his mouth when I wrap my hand around his hard length. He responds with his kiss. I inspect how thick and long he is, how big and round his tip is. He feels silky as I stroke him lightly, and he gets harder. "Do you want me?"

"Yes, but it's not the time. Your hand is soft and perfect, so good touching me." He curses under his breath, "This is a bad idea."

"I can kiss it and make it better."

"Grrrrrr... I'm sure you can, but the first time I'm in you... I will be in control and I won't be in your mouth. There's no way I let my woman go down on me when I haven't made love to her yet, when I haven't been down on her, when I haven't pleasured her to my standards."

I get to his ear, "How about I climb on top of you right here and ride you, Kade?"

"Not helping, didn't bring condoms on purpose."

"I'm clean, I'm on birth control and I've never gone bare. Seems like a good time for a first. You should be my first."

"Fuck, Liv." He pulls me onto his chest and wraps his arms around me tight while he kisses me. He's naked and I still have my shorts and bra on from yesterday. The heat of skin on skin, the feel of him against me, holding me to him, his cock rubbing between my thighs. I want to get him off and I squeeze him with my thighs. "Fuck. Fuck. Fuck. I'm too close for that."

"It's okay, I want you to have what you want."

"I want to come with you and in you, so it's going to have to wait. Fuck, you make me nuts."

"You can always do it again. Seems like it will be days before we're together. You aren't ready yet. I didn't mean..." he cut me off.

"Liv, after last night, I know it's right." He smiles at me and I read things in his eyes I've never seen before. "We need to get out of bed, I can't trust myself right now."

"Are you saying you want to take advantage of me?"

He chuckles, "Oh, yeah."

"But, I'm a sweet defenseless girl. What will I ever do?"

"Of all the women I've met, you're the least defenseless. That defenseless Southern Belle routine might be fun after we've been married for years."

I sit up straight, "I'm sorry, what?"

He laughs, "I'm kidding. I'm not into role playing."

"It sounds like you're making plans for me and I'm not making plans or safe choices anymore."

"Who said anything about it being safe? Maybe somebody else should make plans and decisions for you."

"Again, what?"

He laughs at me this time, "I'm playing with you, baby." He sits up and grabs me, bringing me back to his mouth and kissing me silly. Everything floats away except Kade, his mouth and his hands on me. I don't understand how he takes me away from the rest of the world like this, but I love it.

He pulls his underwear back on and a pair of shorts. He reaches for his shirt and I protest.

"You should leave your shirt off, don't you think? It's simply a waste of time to put your shirt on. Honestly, it's an injustice." I examine his chest and realize I may have had more fun last night than I thought, having left a hickey on his chest and a bruise from my teeth on his shoulder.

"Are you going to leave your shirt off?"

"Oh, no, I wish I could, but it's that damn double standard. It's not socially acceptable for a woman to go shirtless. I'll remember to toss my bikini in my bag next time."

"This bra looks like a bikini top."

"Yes, but it could easily come off or fall open with just a slight action and you don't want that to happen, do you?"

"I'd love that," he chuckles.

I fake shock, "Well, I never."

"Hhmmm... Then maybe it's time you did."

"What do you have in mind sailor?" Before I can take another breath, Kade is kissing down my neck to my chest and kissing my cleavage, licking between my breasts. "Oh, you really can't be trusted. Am I supposed to be the voice of reason? You know where I stand on making safe choices. Isn't getting me naked part of the gift you're waiting for?"

He kisses my lips sweetly, "Yes."

I turn my back to him, "I'm sure you'd like the view, but..." I unhook my bra in the back to give him a teasing view and his hands come around me instantly cupping my breasts from behind.

"You belong in my hands," his voice full of intent.

"Bad boy. This was a look and don't touch scenario."

"There's no way that's going to happen." I get my bra back on before he takes it off completely.

"Obviously, I need to wear a shirt." I say decisively as I pull my shirt on and he fake pouts at me. "It doesn't mean you should put your shirt on, to be clear."

"Yes, ma'am."

He opens all the curtains and climbs into the front seat. "Grab that bag and we can eat breakfast on the drive back."

I fasten myself into the front seat and open the bag to find donut holes, many with nuts. We stop at the outpost for coffee and I buy a tank top, screen printed with, "I'd rather be chillin' with the moon and stars at Celestial Park" and a crescent moon with cartoon character features gazing at the stars. We climb back into the bus and as soon as I have Kade's full attention, I hop out and pull my shirt off right in front of the outpost on the mountain road.

"Liv, what are you doing?"

"Isn't it obvious?"

"Not unless you're stripping in a parking lot."

"I'm changing my shirt."

He leans his head back, shaking it, "Get on with it and let's get out of here. I don't like sharing what's mine."

I pull my new tank top on. "What's yours?"

He groans, but stays quiet and I laugh. I sit sideways, watching him while he drives home and taking control of the music. He does everything with confidence and exudes sexy driving the old Volkswagen wearing only his cargo shorts. I lean my head against the back of the seat. "Did you see any shooting stars?"

"Yeah, they were cool. I'm hoping I caught them with one of the cameras."

"I missed them."

"You were asleep on my chest and I had my arm around you. It was perfect."

"Did you make a wish?"

"Yeah."

"I made a wish, too."

"You said you didn't see a shooting star."

"I wished on the first star. You know? Like the nursery rhyme."

"What did you wish for?"

"I can't tell you. I'm not going to jinx myself."

"What if I can make your dream come true?"

"You're not a magic genie. I can't tell you what I want and poof."

"Fair enough, I guess wishes will come true or they won't."

"I think wishes are like a suggestion to whatever determines our path, like if we can, take a right at the fork in the road. I've never really considered wishes before though, because I've always made the safe choice." I look directly at him, "I made a real wish last night."

He parks in front of his office and gets out of the van, walking around to get his equipment from the back and stops at my door. He opens my door, turns me to him, and wraps his arms around me. His eyes wide and clear, the gold flecks dancing like flames. "I made a real wish, too," I smile at him uncontrollably, like a fool. He leans in pressing his lips to mine and pulls me against him. He wraps my leg around him and deepens the kiss. His warm soft lips dragging across mine and his tongue teasing me until I go after his, lightly sucking on it. My hands back on his chest again and his hands holding me to him, not letting go. Both of us on ragged breaths, "How do we keep ending up here? We have no control."

"I like it. Control is safe and I'm done with safe."

He chuckles under his breath, "You take my control away." Rough at my ear, "I need you." He takes a breath, "I want you wrapped around me. I want to kiss you everywhere. I want to make you shake in pleasure." He stops and looks at me, he has more to say or maybe things he wants to show me.

He runs his hands through his hair and steps back. He gets his equipment and runs it upstairs. He's back quickly and ready to go. "Lunch? Home? Batting cages? What's next?"

"You should probably take me home."

"Probably, but I don't want to."

"I don't want you to either, but I need to change and get ready so I can go to your place tonight."

"I don't want to leave you there alone. I know you can take care of yourself, but I'm not taking any chances."

"Which one is it? You want me with you or you want me safe?"

"Both, and trust me they don't go together. I need you safe, so I can have you."

"What do you mean *have me*?"

A low groan echoes through him, "I'll give you a demonstration. Not something I can explain in words."

"Give it a shot."

"Fuck, Liv. It's more like you'll have me, all of me. I'll give you everything."

"You should definitely take me home," the nerves are taking my body over. It's different now, he's ready. I want him, but now it's real and my fear of not being good enough is making me nauseas.

"What?"

"It's okay, I can walk from here." I reach for the door handle and he stops me.

"No." He starts the van and backs out of the parking space before I can get out. "I'll take you home if that's what you want."

I face out the passenger window, ignoring him. I'm shaky and sweating. I'm in my head. It's going to be like having sex for the first time. He's a master with his fingers, better than anything I've ever had. He's passionate and he loves me, though I'm waiting to hear the words. Wait, does he love me? None of them have ever really loved me. Mark would say it sometimes, but only because he wanted sex. How do I know he loves me? I don't know what it feels like. I've got no experience. Kade's right, it's not logical.

"Liv?"

"Yeah?" I answer still looking away from him.

He reaches for me, touching my shoulder. His whole tone changes, "We're almost home." He parks and runs around to me, opening the door and embracing me. "You're trembling and clammy. What happened?" He asks holding me and not letting go. I don't know if he's not taking any chances on me running from him or worried about me.

"Nothing."

"You gotta talk to me."

"It got real."

He whispers in my ear sweetly, "I want it to be real. Do you want it to be real?"

I nod, but can't speak.

"You've been pushing for sex and wanting me all week. I want you, I needed to make sure you want me for the right reasons. I don't want you to run from me..." his voice softens, "I need you more than I needed her and I can't do that again." He brings my mouth to his and kisses me sweetly. "It's okay if you're not ready. Let's get you upstairs."

I stop him and whisper in his ear, "You said you loved her. How did you know?"

He takes a deep breath, "It's not logical, Liv. There's not a straight answer. I wanted to be with her all the time. It was physically impossible to be as happy as I was with her when she wasn't with me. She felt like she belonged in my hands. The outside world would evaporate around me and I'd only be able to see, feel, her. I'd get jealous and protective. When we were alone together nothing else mattered. I could feel it in my chest. The way our bodies reacted to each other. I was worried I'd never have that again, but I'm not anymore."

His happy eyes dim as memories pass through his head, "Sorry, I didn't mean to be bringing up the past."

"It's okay, it's part of my life," his face twists up, like he's trying to figure out why I asked, "Don't worry about her. It's been over a long time."

I hadn't even considered her, "Nobody has ever loved me."

"I'm sure they have. You just weren't aware of it. Love can hit you all at once and after it hits you, you know the special person loves you, too." He stops and looks at me, and I wonder if he's putting the pieces together, "You're not shaking anymore."

"What if it's different after we have sex?"

"It will be. It will be better. It will make us closer."

That sounds like a guy answer, "Can we not have sex when I stay over tonight?"

"Whatever you want. You tell me when."

"Okay."

He carries my tote and my bat up the stairs for me. I'm right behind him when he stops me, "The door is locked, but coming off at the jamb. Let me check it out first."

"Kade, I'm sure it's nothing."

"Humor me." He unlocks the door and wanders through my apartment. "Okay, come on in. I don't see anything strange, but the door isn't secure. Pack up everything you need because I'm not leaving you here alone. I can stay here with you, if you would prefer."

He's serious and I'm not going to question him protecting me. Everything starts to click. He has been protecting me. My body reacts to him without me. We always want to be together. When I'm with him the rest of the world disappears. Everything is right when I'm with him and nothing else has ever mattered as much. I get warm all over at the epiphany and my smile spreads across my cheeks. "Your place is fine."

"What's got you so happy all of the sudden? I like it. I can see it in your eyes."

"I'm catching up. Give me a few minutes to pack, okay?"

"Take as long as you need."

"You said everything I need, right?"

"Yes. Girlie shower stuff and whatever."

"Okay." I pull out my biggest piece of luggage and empty my tote. I put all my toiletries in the tote bag and pack the big suitcase full of my favorite t-shirts, underwear, work clothes, jeans, sweats—everything I wear on a regular basis. I toss the shoes I need in on top of my toiletries and grab my old James Blunt T-shirt, tossing it in at the last minute. I pack up my laptop, e-reader and charging cables. I walk out to the living room with my electronics bag slung over my shoulder, tote in my hand and dragging my suitcase behind me. "I'm ready."

Kade looks up at me, laughingly, "Did you pack enough?"

"I'm not sure how many days it will take for my door to get fixed and you don't want me here until it's safe. I'm not too concerned, but I'll go along with it for you. Your place is probably more dangerous for me, but I'm not making decisions based on safety anymore."

"I like it, commitment."

"Are you sure about this?"

"I've never been more sure about anything."

"Okay, because it's not appropriate to have sex with your roommate," I try my hardest to keep a straight face.

He looks at me shaking his head, immediately getting up and walking over to me. "It's a good thing you aren't my roommate then because you will be sleeping in my bed and I want you." He scoops me up into his arms and I automatically wrap my legs around him while he kisses me. I kiss him back and there's a heat between us, the magnetic pull strong and needy pulling us together. I stop and take a deep breath, gazing at him. "Liv, is it too much? Do you feel it?"

"The heat drawing us together?"

"Yeah, you feel it. Good. I don't want to be alone in this."

"Alone in what? What is this?"

"Let's go, baby." He takes my luggage from me and locks the door behind us, leading me down the stairs and back to the bus.

He drives a few blocks and turns a corner toward the old downtown. A garage door opens and he pulls in next to an old Camaro. "This is my place. I want you to make yourself at home." He kisses me and leads me into the house. It's not a small one-bedroom apartment like my place. No, it's a real house with multiple bedrooms, a home office, a spacious kitchen, a family room, two bathrooms and a yard in the back with a big tree.

"It's a great place. Is it only you here?"

"Yes, I know I don't need this much space, but I like the house."

"Where should I put my stuff?"

He takes my suitcase and leads me into the master suite. "There's room in the closet for you to hang up your clothes, the bathroom is that door..." he walks over to his dresser and combines his T-shirts and underwear down to two drawers instead of four, "...and these two drawers are yours. I'll work on clearing out room for you, but this should do for now. There's two sinks in the bathroom, just claim the one that's not used. Oh, and the nightstand on your side is empty."

I take a couple steps backwards, listening to him and absorbing my surroundings.

"Forget all that." He says and pulls me against him. "All that matters is you're here with me."

He's reading me and doesn't want me to freak out. It's a lot and I'm only visiting, but his words and actions make it seem like it's permanent or will be. He keeps the afternoon and evening low key, ordering delivery for dinner. We sit together comfortably in his bed while I read and he works on his laptop. I unpack my clothes, shoes and toiletries, taking the space in his closet and showing my presence in his bathroom. I disappear into the bathroom to shower and I set some music to play on my phone. The shower is perfect, warm and massaging on my neck and back. I wash my hair and appreciate how I'm going to leave his bathroom smelling all tropical and girlie. I dry off and tie my hair up in a knot. Needing my creature comforts, I pull on my worn out concert shirt with the holes and my cutoff sweats. I find Kade napping and crawl into his bed with him, resting my head on his chest.

CHAPTER 10

I wake up in the middle of the night, it's dark and the chest I love to sleep on is missing. I check my surroundings without getting out of bed and remember I'm at Kade's. I hear a noise in the other room. My shorts are twisted and uncomfortable, so I drop them in my sleepy state and go looking for him. I find him in the kitchen getting a drink and walk directly to him, wrapping my arms around his neck and kissing him with need. I need him. I nibble on his lips and suck on his tongue, while my fingers play with the short length of his hair. "My chest was gone." I move my hands to his chest and kiss it.

"Your chest?"

"Yeah, I love you, so its mine," still half asleep.

"Logic I can get behind. You must be mine then, because I love you. Let's go back to bed, baby."

I giggle happily. Suddenly my feet are off the floor and he's carrying me back to the bedroom. My legs wrapped around Kade tightly, I can't help but move against him. I kiss his neck, hot and open-mouthed.

"Liv, you only have a T-shirt and panties on."

"Uh-huh."

"Do you want to put your shorts back on?"

"No."

Kade sits down on the edge of the bed with his feet on the floor and I end up straddling his lap. I lock eyes with him while my hands travel his body from his shoulders to his waist. I unbutton and unzip his cargo shorts, and I pull my T-shirt off.

"Fuck me. Liv, baby..."

"I'm yours, Kade," I focus on him wide-eyed, begging him to show me—everything.

His whole attitude changes and his hands on me become protective. Chivalrously showing how much he cares about me, and not holding back. Handling me with such care, like he's afraid I'll break. He stands, picking me up with him and lies me down on his bed. He drops his cargo shorts to the floor and sends his boxer briefs with them. He stands at the foot of the bed, "You're so beautiful." I push my panties off while he watches me, giving myself completely. He crawls up next to me, both of us naked with heat emanating from us. He leans over me, gazing deep into my eyes and kisses me tenderly. "I want you more than anything. Only you, Liv. You own me." His honesty and his heart in his smile, as it creeps up to his eyes. His warm hands caressing my skin leave a trail of fire, while he kisses me tenderly and deepens our connection. He drags a line of kisses from my mouth to my breasts and squeezes them gently while be licks my nipples sending heat shooting through my body. It pulls at my sex and I arch off the bed. He sucks at my nipple drawing my breast into his mouth and I reach for his hard cock, needing him. "Not yet, baby," he says and rubs against me.

"Please, Kade. I need you."

He kisses my belly down to my navel and lies between my legs. He kisses the inside of my thigh and my body tenses in anticipation of what will happen next. My ass in his hands, he lifts me to his mouth. His hot, wet mouth is on me, licking me and sucking at me. I arch off the bed again uncontrollably. He buries his tongue deeper. "You're so sweet, baby." His luxurious tongue teases me, bringing me closer to ecstasy. "I need to be in you. I need to feel your love. I want you and you're not ready for me yet, baby. Tell me you want me."

"I want to feel you slide into me. I want us together. I need you inside me. You're the key to my world. Everything is right when I have you with me and nothing else exists. It's just us. I want you, every part of you."

He slides his finger in me, pulling a whimper from my lips. "Oh fuck you're tight, Liv." He strokes me with his finger and starts licking my clit. His tongue is my end, every piece of me being fixated on the skillful movement of his tongue. I buck and he stops. "No, baby. We need to get you ready for me before you come." He slides a second finger in, stretching me and pounding into me harder and harder. Everything he does takes me to another level of pleasure, pushing my need and desire, and proving to me he is where I belong.

I cry out his name and he latches on to my clit, sucking hard while he continues to stroke me with his fingers. I scream out as I'm flying off into the stars and can't control my own body. My eyes flutter closed as I reach for him, any part of him. "Kade, please."

"I've got you, Liv." His mouth is on mine kissing me sweetly, he moves to my neck and whispers in my ear, "I love you," with such sincerity happy tears fall from my eyes as he pushes into me for the first time and my heartbeat quickens. He wraps his arms around me, "Little at a time, baby." He pushes a little further with each stroke. I'm not prepared for how thick and long he is.

"More. I want all of you. Please, Kade," my voice is filled with a need I've never heard before.

He cradles my head, kissing me sweetly while he continues to move slow.

"I need you. I need you to give me all of you."

"I can't. I'll hurt you." He kisses my cheek.

"It doesn't matter. I need you. I need to have you. I need you to love me all the way."

"Fuck." He holds me tightly to him with arms wrapped completely around me, nothing could separate us. He presses his soft lips to mine, open mouthed and needy. He drives my need and my body moves with him, meeting his every stroke. His heart racing, "I need you, too." He groans low and in need, like he's been starving. His grip tightens and he forces himself the rest of the way into me, slamming me over and over.

I scream out and he muffles my cries with his kiss. All I can do is appreciate his pleasure, like thunder inside me after the lightning strike. All man, thick and hard. The blood rushing in my ears. He moves in me slower. "Is there more?"

"You have all of me, baby," he smiles, content with himself.

"I need you. I need all of you. I can feel your heart. You're beyond what I imagined in my dreams. Thicker, longer, you're everything." Having all of him brings him into my center. His hands warm on my skin become more possessive, leaving a path of tingles in their wake. "Is it real? Do you love me?" I know in my heart he does and I want to hear the words again.

He holds his hard length deep inside me and gazes into my eyes, "I feel you in my heart and see you when my eyes are closed. I hear your voice in everything around me and your laugh tickles me like a breeze blowing through me. You fulfill my soul and make me whole. You make my heart warm and my body feel like it's finally in focus." Kade's voice thick with emotion, he leans his forehead to mine. "I need you to breathe. I love you because I don't know any words that mean more."

He starts taking long slow strokes in and out, over and over, dragging across my sensitive nub with every pass. My body is a live-wire, sensitive to everything. Every stroke pushing me closer to my end and making my body spark. Our bodies take over, pushing and pulling, needing each other more with every second that passes.

I cry out with every stroke as the friction and slick heat between us win and I've lost all control. I belong to him. His pleasure is all that matters. I mirror his need and my body is pushing his faster. "Love me harder, Kade," escapes my lips desperately. His fingers dig into me, holding me with need.

"Grrrrr..." He pounds into me harder and harder. His need taking over. He kisses my neck and sits up, as he slams into me, so fucking amazing.

"Oh, Kade. Yes! Oh." My cries push him forward. He spreads my legs farther apart, edging his way in deeper. "Oh, fuck." He pounds into me deep, filling me repeatedly.

He brings my ankles to my ears and whispers while he's buried inside me, "More?"

"Yes." He finds his way deeper, bending me in half for access.

"You're perfect, Liv. So fucking tight around me. Pulling at me like you need me. Squeezing all of me."

"I do need you. I'm yours."

He's moving in me like he can't get close enough to me and I start to move with him. The friction and heat becoming too much. We move together, out of control.

"Oh, Liv. I'm..."

"Please don't stop. Faster, Kade. Please. Oh my... Oh, Kade!" It's primal, both of us on the edge and unable to stop. Crying out in pleasure. I grab for him, needing him against me. He gets harder and larger, needing me and approaching his climax.

He moves faster and I'm lost in darkness, screaming out his name as my body clenches his hard cock. Stars shoot through the darkness as I lose myself in the passion of him taking me as his.

"Liv..." He slams into me hard and he trembles at his release as he collapses on me. His hard cock throbbing inside me as my body continues to shudder around him. He claims my mouth with his, tenderly keeping our connection and holding me. Our bodies melting together as one. Both of us surviving on ragged breaths, "I've got you, Liv. I'll always have you." He holds me close and doesn't let go.

PLAYLIST

"All I Need" by Jack Wagner
"Broken" by Lovelytheband
"Fell in Love With a Girl" by The White Stripes
"It's My Life" by Bon Jovi
"Love Somebody" by Rick Springfield
"Seven Nation Army" by The White Stripes
"Sit Next to Me" by Foster the People
"Someone Singing Along" by James Blunt
"Take My Hand" by Picture This
"When It's Love" by Van Halen
"You Are So Beautiful" by Joe Cocker
"You're Beautiful" by James Blunt

JUST A CALIFORNIA GIRL
BETTING ON LOVE, BOOK 1 (VEGAS ROMANCE)

Who knew I'd meet the love of my life on a girls night in Las Vegas? Definitely not me.

"Remember the moment we're together when I'm your world and nothing else exists. I've never had that with anybody else and I'm willing to bet you haven't either."

Those heartfelt words that fell from his lips have taken residence in my head, crushing my soul since I haven't told him who I am. What if he doesn't want the real me?

Danny's a hunky metal head with soulful brown eyes. His sexy tiger tattoo makes me burn from the inside out. He's everything I want and need.

I want to keep him. But, I can't tell him I love him until I confess my innocuous lie. I wouldn't believe it myself.

Betting on Love... could be the riskiest gamble of all.

THE SWEET SPOT

AN ALL ABOUT THE DIAMOND ROMANCE BOOK 1

Can her baseball fantasy become reality, or will she strike out at love?

Rick Seno is a sexy warrior behind the plate in his catcher's gear. In control and calling the game for the San Diego Seals. He'd show me the same attention in my bed, if he was more than my imaginary baseball boyfriend.

I've worn a Seno jersey to every game since Rick became a big leaguer. It's silly. I'm almost a decade older than him. I don't compare to the flawless baseball skanks who wait for him at the player's garage.

But, what am I supposed to do when the All-Star of my dreams invites me out after a game?

I can't believe he wants me. Until tonight, I was completely content with my life. Now, I'm caught off base and I'm not sure I can make it home safe.

ACKNOWLEDGMENTS

I have a wonderful new community of friends that I didn't expect when I started my romance writing journey, but my original alpha reader will always be the same. She has been there for me through everything. She has supported me in my crazy author moments and listened to me ramble as I wrote my first book. She is my hardest critic. She makes me rewrite chapters. We've brainstormed character names at 2am. Midnight phone calls turn into me staying up all night to write Muffin Man. She's been hounding me to release Kade and Liv for over a year. It's time.

Andie, you will always be the sister I chose.

ABOUT THE AUTHOR

USA Today Bestselling Author Naomi Springthorp is a born and raised Southern California girl. She's a baseball freak who supports her team all season long and blatantly admires the athletes in those pants. Music has always been part of her life and she believes everything has a soundtrack. She loves her two feline fur babies, though they're not quite sure what to do with her.

She writes Baseball Romance, Romantic Comedies, 90s Throwback, and Contemporary Romance--all with heat and sometimes a little sweet.

Join her newsletter at
www.naomispringthorp.com/sign-up

ALSO BY NAOMI SPRINGTHORP

AN ALL ABOUT THE DIAMOND ROMANCE

The Sweet Spot

King of Diamonds

Diamonds in Paradise

Star-Crossed in the Outfield

The Closer

Falling for Prince

Up to Bat

BETTING ON LOVE

Just a California Girl

Jacks

Strings Attached

STANDALONE NOVELS & NOVELLAS

Muffin Man

Finally in Focus

Confessions of an Online Junkie

ANTHOLOGIES & BOX SETS

Sacrifice for Love

Storybook Pub

Storybook Pub Christmas Wishes

Young Crush

Storybook Pub 2

Hate to Want You

Tricks, Treats, & Teasers

Caught Under the Mistletoe

All Access Pass

Made in the USA
Middletown, DE
08 April 2023